# Author's Note

In the coming pages I'm going to share with you a story about a runner named Benson Wilder.

However, it is also not his story.

With that in mind if you only remember one thing for the rest of this story, and even for the rest of your life. Remember this....

That no person's story is theirs alone. Because there is only one true feeling in this world. And that is the feeling we share with those we love.

# IN HER EYES

# Also By Wesley Banks

*Hope In Every Raindrop*

# IN HER EYES

Wesley Banks

In Her Eyes
Copyright © 2016 by Wesley Banks

First Edition: March 2016

ISBN 978-0-9861934-2-2 (e-book)
ISBN 978-0-9861934-3-9 (paperback)

Chasing Pace Publishing

*For my parents who always taught me to never give up.*

# IN HER EYES

# 1

## PROMISE

*June 12, 2015*

The first time he saw her was on a day just like today.

The sky was blue and cloudless, like the color of the ocean from a plane. Waves of bodies swept through the stadium. Some formed endless lines at the scattered concessions, while others made their way through the stands, bumping and nudging one another along. Loudspeakers broadcasted in intervals to the crowd, but laughter and noisy conversations, as well as irritated voices and protests, drowned out the robotic instructions as people pushed their way near the fence for a better view.

All of them were waiting impatiently for the last event of the weekend. The men's 5,000 meter.

Ben tried to drown it all out with the slow and deliberate details of his pre-race warm-up. He stood up and unzipped his jacket, tossing it in his bag below the bench.

A bead of sweat rolled slowly down his neck until it found the edge of his shirt. He pulled the breakaway pants from his hips and laid them atop the jacket. His mental block wavered and for a moment he could hear the crowd begin to chant. The blue and orange letters on several signs appeared as he looked up towards all the people. Then he closed his eyes and looked down at his shoes. He focused on the smallest detail his eye could resolve, counting the fiber of each individual stitching, and the sounds slowly disappeared again.

He continued examining each lace like a surgeon checking sutures. He lifted his left leg and shook it out several times. Then his right. He bounced up and down twice. The shoes felt perfect.

The infield grass flexed underneath his steps as he jogged toward the starting line where the other runners were stretching. He passed them and continued running until he was almost even with turn number four, and then he walked back. Twice more he completed the same routine, shaking out his arms and clinching his hands as he stopped near the starting boxes.

He took several steps forward towards the chalk line etched into the track, knelt down and placed his hand against the clay red polyurethane. It breathed in and out the afternoon sun through its porous surface and refused to flex against the humidity. The track would be fast today.

As he looked up towards the seats, the sound of the stadium returned. He saw a girl making her way up the stands with a slice of pizza and a coke. Her light blonde hair was short, and pulled back in a ponytail the same way Casey wore it. She swept several loose strands behind each ear, and several more fell loose against her neck. Ben couldn't pull his eyes away until she found her seat next to two other girls and sat down. He looked back towards the track, and then once more in the girl's direction, even though he knew it wasn't her. The announcer was trying to draw attention to the triple jump on the south end of the field. But the crowd was waiting anxiously for something else. They inched in around the chest-high black chain link fence that surrounded the track.

Directly across from Ben several security guards pushed a group of frat guys away from the barrier. Just a few feet away from them a young boy with red hair and a ruddy complexion dropped his cup, soda spilling all over the bottom of his legs and feet. His father jerked him away from the fence, the large plastic souvenir cup rolling quietly on the ground, alone.

A heavy hand on his shoulder startled him, pulling him away from his thoughts. "How you feelin', kid?"

Coach Melvick stood just a few feet behind him. Their conversation from this morning still weighed heavily on Ben. He had run one way for as long as he could remember, and the morning of the most important race of his life, Coach Melvick had asked him to change everything. It wasn't just the change that burdened him though. It was the impossibility of it all. "Ask me again with a thousand meters left."

Coach turned his head and stared off into the distance. Without looking at Ben, he asked, "You ever watch the Nature Channel?"

The random question caught Ben off guard. "Umm, no, not really. Why?"

"I love that damn channel. Chocked full of interesting stuff." Coach paused again and his eyes seemed to wander towards the stands.

"The other day I was watching this documentary on wolves. You probably wouldn't think it, but they are

3

absolutely fucking magnificent long distance runners." He paused again. "You know how they figured that out?"

Ben shook his head again not entirely sure what this had to do with anything.

"They chased the damn thing with a snowmobile just to see how far it could go. Now, if I was that wolf, I would have turned around and chewed their sorry faces off. But this wolf must have been one cocky SOB, because he just kept running. Those idiots followed him for hours, until eventually they had to turn around. But that damn wolf just kept on running…"

Coach looked down at Ben now. "You know how he did it?"

Again Ben just shook his head.

"He did it the same way you do anything in life, by putting one damn foot in front of the other." Coach Melvick's eyes burned into Ben and then without another word he walked towards the infield with the rest of his team.

\* \* \*

Coach Melvick sat down on a wooden bench painted with the green and yellow colors of the Oregon Ducks. He pulled out a half-smoked cigar and held it between his lips while he struck a match across the glass powder surface until the phosphorus and air created a small flame. He spun the cigar around in the modest orange light and then tossed the expired match onto the ground next to him. He smiled as he took the cigar out of his mouth for a second, examining the tip he had just primed.

Then his smile faded as he thought about the wolf, the hopeless expression on the animals face when he realized he could never outrun the guys on the snowmobile. After about four hours, the wolf had collapsed. That amazing animal ran his heart out, literally.

\* \* \*

The starting judge walked from runner to runner. When he reached Ben he said the same thing he said to the other twenty-three guys. "Five minutes 'till start."

"Ladies and Gentlemen," the loud speakers boomed. "The last event of the 2015 NCAA Division 1 Outdoor Track & Field Championships will begin in five minutes. Please take your seats."

As the roaring cheer erupted behind Ben, two young brunette trainers walked by. The water bottles on their hips swishing alongside a blue fanny pack that hung around their khaki shorts. They both had their hair pulled up in ponytails. The girl on the left was wearing one of those bracelets made from old parachute cord. Both smiled as they walked up to him. "Good luck today, Ben."

He smiled back as the one on the left adjusted her ponytail, arching her back as she pushed the hair band tighter against her head. Her bracelet flashed in the sun revealing a metal clasp holding two ends of the cord together. On the clasp were several letters he couldn't make out.

Her name was Jane or Jeanne, or something with a J. "You need anything?"

It was the same damn question she always asked. He wanted to lean forward and spell it out for her. *No. I. Don't. Need. Anything. From. You.* Instead he smiled, and politely declined.

Several runners walked into his line of sight, as the girls walked back towards the other end of the field. They began to casually stretch, rolling their wrists and ankles to shake away the nerves more than to loosen their muscles and joints. And then Kevin Robinson walked by.

"Looking a little pale today, Benny boy."

Kevin Robinson was the number one ranked 5000-meter runner in NCAA Division 1. The only runner ranked above Ben. He was your prototypical college asshole. Blond hair, blue eyes, tanned like a surfer instead of a runner, rich parents, and a full ride to USC. It didn't hurt that he also held the fastest 5000-meter time this year.

This should have been the second time they raced in the same heat, except that Kevin had been pulled from a meet earlier in the year due to disciplinary reasons. Something about him having skipped a week of practice for a trip with the girls' soccer team. There were always rumors like that about him floating around.

They had never technically met, but ranking one and two with only a few points separating them, both knew of each other even though they attended schools across the country. Ben tried to look right through Kevin as he walked up to the starting boxes. But Coach's words from this morning made it tough.

Kevin stopped in lane five, two lanes from Ben. "You sure you're feeling up to this today? I hear the heat can really get to the elderly." Most of the other runners were focused, still stretching, or loosening up. But several smirked at Kevin's joke.

Kevin was a twenty-two-year-old senior, while Ben was a twenty-four year-old freshman. It wasn't the first time he had heard a joke about his age.

Ben looked over at Kevin, staring straight into his eyes until the screams and shouts of several girls from along the fence stole his attention.

"Ben! Ben!" the girls shouted.

He looked over to see several girls holding a glitter laden poster that read: "Ben, Ben, Ben! Win, Win, Win!" It was some of the girls from Alpha Omega Pi, or AOGuy as they were referred to on campus. Not in any way because of their looks, they were gorgeous, but they just also happened to dominate intramural sports.

Kevin shook his head sarcastically as the starting judge approached and all twenty-four runners took their position.

"Don't worry," Kevin said. "It will all be over soon. For you and your fan club," he said laughing.

Those last words didn't register with Ben because he was still thinking about Kevin's previous remark. Not that it bothered him. Just that he began to think about the past few months all over again.

"Runners, on your mark."

Ben didn't move, as the others crouched slightly and shifted their weight onto their front foot.

"Runners, get set." He was still lost in thought as the others tightened, bringing their arms up like a boxer into ready position.

The gun fired, and his body instinctively went into motion, but all he could think about was the two girls he loved more than anything. And the one promise he had to keep, if he didn't die first.

# 2

## A Girl Named Casey

*3 months earlier*

*March 31, 2015*

Ben dropped his backpack by his desk, walked over to his twin bed and fell face first onto the dark navy sheets.

Differential equations, strength of materials, and dynamics back-to-back-to-back every Monday, Wednesday, and Friday morning. The joys of being a mechanical engineering major. Having been a mechanic straight out of high school for about five years, the concepts were easy to grasp. But the sheer number of equations alone literally hurt his brain.

He lay there for a few more minutes and then decided he didn't want to waste the rest of his Friday.

Ben sat up on the edge of his bed and ran his fingers over his eyes. He put his palm under his chin and twisted his neck left, and then right, making several cracking sounds.

Parker was lying on his stomach sound asleep on the bed across the room. His left arm was hanging over the side, and the sheets looked like someone had tried to tie them in a giant knot.

Parker and Ben were suite mates at the Springs Complex. It was essentially a studio apartment, except no kitchen, and they shared a bathroom. They each had their own bed, desk, chair, and what the university expects people to believe is a closet.

Ben's side of the room was mostly empty except for a black and white poster of Steve Prefontaine with words in thick white letters written on it: "Most people run a race to see who is the fastest. I run a race to see who has the most guts."

Parker's wall was different, covered in posters of half-naked girls, and a cork board pinned full of drunken moments.

After walking on to the team, Ben was offered a full scholarship to keep running at the University of Florida. A lot of the athletes dormed here because they were on scholarship. They weren't the best dorms on campus, but they weren't the worst either.

Ben thought back to the light blue house on Citrus Drive, right next to Forest High School. The mailbox outside that looked like a bird house, and the handprints made in wet concrete when they fixed a block on the sidewalk. It had become so lonely and quiet. He looked around the dorm room again. These dorms, they were his new home.

Ben pulled the blinds open and the late morning sun washed over the room with a phalanx of yellow rays.

Parker made a noise that sounded more like a cat dying than a person waking up.

"Rise and shine, sunshine," Ben said.

Parker made another indistinguishable sound.

"I'm going to go for a short run and stop by Broward Dining for some lunch. You want to go?"

Parker finally responded with actual words. "No, man, I'm good."

"All right, I should be back in a few hours."

\* \* \*

A myriad of numbers and equations were still floating around Ben's mind, but the sun felt good against his skin as he ran.

He jogged for about an hour. At first away from campus down Museum Road, and then back toward campus up Hull and Mowry. He took a left on Gale Lemerand, passing the empty parking lot normally filled with giant RVs during football season, and then a right back on Museum Road in front of the Physics Lawn that was mostly empty.

He jogged up the slight incline in front of the campus theater, which he couldn't recall the name of, and ended up in front of the Reitz Union.

A small group of students that he didn't recognize said, "Hey," as he passed, and a guy from another group shouted, "Good luck against Missouri," which made absolutely zero sense because the meet this weekend was in Texas and Missouri wasn't even one of the schools invited.

Ben just raised his hand in acknowledgment and mouthed the words, "Thanks, man," as he passed.

He'd been receiving a lot of attention ever since he broke the school record during the first meet of the season, and then the conference record during the Texas Relays last weekend.

It wasn't going over well with some of the guys on the team who thought he was showboating, but he didn't really care.

Ben looked over to his right as he passed McCarty Hall and then felt a strange metallic crunch under his foot. He stopped running and looked down at the sidewalk, several beads of sweat running across his face. He bent over and picked up a pair of keys and a light gray UF ID card that belonged to "Casey Taylor…"

"Thank you," he heard before he could finish reading the name on the card.

He looked up to see a girl drawing in a couple of sharp, labored breaths. She had light blonde hair just long enough for a ponytail, several strands falling away on each side of her face. Her left hand was resting on her hip as her right hung loose at her side. She was wearing gray cotton shorts that were slightly curled at the ends, like they had been cut from a pair of sweatpants. Her top was a light purple color and clung tightly to a bright pink sports bra despite the outline of a heart rate monitor beneath.

"I think those are mine," she said, pointing to the keys that Ben was still holding.

His eyes followed the soft tan that stretched over her body.

Ben brushed the card against his shorts, wiping it clean, and handed both the card and keys to her. "Sorry, I kind of stepped on them."

She tucked the key fob below the elastic waistband of her shorts and held onto the card. "Thanks again," she said, motioning a slight wave goodbye.

11

"You don't like to listen to music when you run?" Ben blurted out.

She squinted her eyes. "What?"

"Music," Ben said again. "I just noticed you're not listening to any."

"Oh, umm, no, I just kind of prefer to get lost in my thoughts."

"Me too," he said. "It just helps…" He paused looking for the right word.

"Quiet things down a bit," she finished.

Ben smiled. "Exactly." He stepped forward and held out his hand. "I'm Ben." Before she could respond, a girl on rollerblades came whirling into him, arms flailing.

Casey stepped back as Ben caught her.

"Oh my gosh. I'm so sorry," the girl said. She tried to right her balance, but as she moved backwards she almost fell again.

Ben grabbed her arms, steadying her. "You okay?"

The girl looked up and smiled at him. "Yeah. I think."

Ben moved away and towards Casey, still standing there watching everything unfold. "Okay, well…"

"Hey, aren't you Benson Wilder?" the girl said. She waved over another girl also on roller blades.

"Uhh, yeah," he said, looking back over at Casey. "Just call me Ben, though, please"

The two girls were now completely blocking him from Casey. "Oh my gosh. We were at your last race. You are so fast."

Casey laughed lightly and then started to turn away again.

Ben put his arm on the girl's shoulder in front of him. "It was great meeting you, but I need to…" He saw her step into a light jog. "Wait."

Casey looked back briefly, but kept moving in the other direction.

"Can I get your number? Your email? Your name?"

She held up the card. "You have my name," she said with a smile. Then she jogged away.

The two girls were talking between each other and then looked at him and asked, "Don't you have a race this weekend against Missouri?"

He just stood there, shaking his head.

# 3

## Girls

Eddie Clark and Jimmy Garcia stood up from the table. Eddie ran hurdles and Jimmy was a sprinter. They both leaned over and bumped fists with Parker. When they looked towards Ben, he took a sip of his drink and ignored them.

"Alright, Parker, we'll catch you later."

"Alright, guys," Parker said. He looked over at Ben after they were out of earshot. "Why do you do that shit?"

"They don't deserve to even be here," Ben said as he watched them make their way through the maze of tables. "They don't take it seriously."

"No one takes it seriously compared to you," Parker said.

"Whatever, man, let's go." Ben stood up and walked his tray over to the trash cans along the wall and Parker followed.

Parker looked right at him as he turned around. "Holy shit, are you still caught up on this girl?"

Ben didn't respond. He just swung the door open and exited the Reitz Union. They both headed down twenty or so

14

steps until they were walking across the north lawn. Hundreds of students were scattered across several acres of grass. Some were in bathing suits on their beach towels, silently affirming the fact that they attended the University of Florida for nothing more than a good tan and an increased shot at skin cancer. Meanwhile, others were simply lying against their backpacks, thankful for the shade of the huge laurel oaks. Sidewalks crisscrossed the cropped lawn, where even more students stood in groups talking, or hurried in directions likely opposite of the class they should be attending.

Parker was finishing off the last of his fourth Subway cookie. He ate it in two bites, as if he hadn't also just had a foot-long meatball sub and about a gallon of soda.

Ben just shook his head. Parker was about three inches taller than him and twenty pounds lighter, regardless of what he ate. He looked the part of a collegiate runner. His DNA was the thing runners dreamed of. Only problem was he didn't actually care that much about running. He was here on scholarship too, but running more or less got in the way of everything else for him. And by everything else, that pretty much just meant girls.

"So, what am I supposed to do now?" Ben asked.

Either Parker was ignoring him or he was busy checking out anything with a skirt and legs. Most likely the latter.

"Earth to Parker."

Parker pried his eyes away from a tan blonde with a low cut top. "What? Yeah, I heard you."

"And...?" Ben said.

"And...nothing. We'll probably pass twenty more blondes on the way to class. Just pick one."

15

He wasn't entirely wrong. A few seconds later another cute girl walked by and Parker nearly tripped as he jerked his head around. Parker looked over at Ben with raised eyebrows. "See what I mean? Why are you so hung up on this girl anyways? You talked to her for what, a few minutes?"

"I don't know man, it's…it's …she was just like gravity."

"Gravity?"

"I don't know how else to describe it. I just feel this pull."

"Holy shit man, you sound like Nicholas Sparks."

"Who?" Ben asked.

"Nicholas Sparks. You know, *The Notebook*, *The Last Song*, *The Longest Ride…*" Parker stopped talking when he saw Ben laughing.

"Do you like to get in your jammies with a bowl of ice cream and cuddle with your cat while you read love stories?"

"Sometimes I hate you."

"I'm picturing it now. It's so cute," Ben joked.

The sidewalk forked to the right and Ben turned towards McCarty Hall. "See you at practice?" Ben asked.

"Unfortunately," Parker said

Ben kept walking towards Carleton Auditorium, but all he could think about was Casey Taylor.

# 4

## CAMOUFLAGE

*April 2, 2015*

By the time he got there, all the lights were turned off in the auditorium full of about four hundred students. He found an empty spot towards the back left. Looking around, he noticed half of the students were at least making an attempt to watch the video about camouflage among animals in nature. The other half were either scrolling mindlessly through Instagram or drooling on their backpack as they slept. Wildlife Studies was probably the stupidest class in the history of college classes.

Everyone took it because it satisfied three of the required six "B" credits, which stood for biological studies. Most people think that colleges make some freshman classes difficult to weed out those who can't cut it. The opposite is actually true. They make some classes so incredibly easy to weed out those who would be better off not wasting the best four years of their life learning about camouflaged frogs.

He tried to join some of the other students and pulled up Instagram on his phone. When Parker had found out Ben wasn't on social media, he set up Ben's Instagram and Facebook. Apparently those are must haves for looking up hot girls you meet—and to give Parker credit, as soon as his account went active, he quickly racked up hundreds of followers, most of them girls. Still, he thought back to all the stupid stuff Parker did. He couldn't believe he was actually following advice from a guy who once ran a race with two left shoes.

He started to type her name into the search field, but the kid next to him hit Ben's arm with a stack of papers. Ben looked over at the kid, a little confused.

"Take one and pass it on, man."

Ben grabbed the stack, taking the top sheet off before passing the stack to the girl on his left. He looked down at the paper in front of him, focusing on the bold black letters at the top of the page that read "QUIZ."

*Shit.*

For a moment he was a little nervous. Then he read the first question.

"Animals use camouflage in the wild as a defense mechanism. True or False?"

*Like I was saying, weed out class.*

# 5

## FACEBOOK

*April 2, 2015*

Parker unlocked the door to their dorm room, and Ben walked in behind him.

"I can't believe we're still talking about this girl," Parker said.

"Just help me look for like ten minutes. If she's not on Facebook or Instagram or whatever other social media crap you have on your phone, then I'll stop talking about her. Deal?"

Parker thought about it for a minute. "No."

"No? Seriously?"

Parker tossed his backpack on the floor and it slid underneath his desk. "If I help you," he paused, "then you owe me."

"Okay, whatever."

Parker sat down at Ben's desk, pulled up Instagram on his laptop, and punched in her name: Casey Taylor. Thank goodness for IDs.

"There are fifty-one Casey Taylor's on Instagram. Most of them are 'private,' though."

"What does that mean?"

"It means you can scan through these tiny-ass profile pictures, but that's it."

Ben leaned over his shoulder while Parker scrolled through them.

"Well?" Parker asked.

Ben's eyes scanned down the center of the page over each of the circular profile pictures in the drop-down menu. Not a single one was the right Casey Taylor. "None of them are her," he said.

"Alright, let's try something else." Parker switched to Facebook and typed in her name again. There were only twenty-two results, and more than half were spelled "Cassey" or "Kasey." Of the seven remaining there was a freelance photographer, a manager of relations, a musician, a host of some weird television show, and then staring back at Ben, a doctor.

Ben pointed to the screen. "Holy cow, that's her."

Ben watched as Parker clicked on her picture. A little box on the left popped up that read:

> *Studied medicine at University of California.*
> *Graduated in 2014.*
> *Lives in Gainesville, FL.*
> *Born March 23, 1990.*
> *Work. Ask to see info.*

"Can we ask to see info?" Ben asked.

Parker looked back and laughed at him. "That's not really how that works, man."

"Okay, well, then it's pretty dumb to put that button there."

"I have so much to teach you young Padawan…" Parker said.

The rest of her profile was pretty empty. Parker explained that she hadn't updated her timeline in several years, which meant she probably forgot she was even on Facebook. It didn't matter, though; at least he had a starting point of how to find Casey Taylor.

# 6

## SHANDS

Including college residents, Shands Hospital has almost one thousand physicians and over eight thousand nurses. How did Ben know this? Because for the last two days he felt as if he'd talked to nearly every one of them. And because it said it on the giant plaque he was standing in front of.

There was a cancer center, a heart care center, women's services, neuromedicine specialties, orthopedics, emergency medicine, radiology, and urology just to name a few.

To put it bluntly. Shands Hospital was fucking huge.

He was surprised he'd even made it through so many hospital wings without the slightest question of who he was or why he was asking about a resident physician named Casey Taylor. He was sure by now there were posters of him all over the place with eight simple words written on them: "Do not talk to this kid; he's crazy."

He stopped a few steps outside the building in front of a giant blue board that read, "UF Health is Baby Friendly." He looked up at the red, blue, purple, and yellow checkered windows that rose for 10 floors. He was at the last place he wanted to be: Shands Children's Hospital.

For a moment he considered just forgetting about the whole thing. This girl had said, what, two sentences to him?

For all he knew there could be posters of her around school that read: "Do not talk to this girl; she's crazy."

He laughed to himself, thinking how Parker would rephrase that. "The crazier, the better."

After about two hours of walking around the hospital, Ben was no closer to finding her than he was two days ago.

What he could describe of Casey ended up describing about thirty percent of the women that worked there, which was nearly three thousand women. That wasn't helpful at all. And that was just from the people that would actually talk to him. Most of them either looked at him like they were about to call security, or they just ignored him completely.

Ben walked by several rooms that looked exactly how he remembered them. Eggshell colored hospital beds were covered with crisp white sheets, tucked neatly at every side. Teddy bears and other stuffed animals lined the beds, and colorful animal balloons floated in front of the health monitors. Most of them also had a navy couch with wood trim that folded into a bed just below the prison like windows. He hated those rooms.

Turning the corner he found the same tiled mural of butterflies, and birds, and dolphins on the wall. And then he heard a familiar voice. A voice he really didn't want to hear.

"Benson?" Dr. Sanchez called out.

The voice stopped Ben cold where he stood. For a moment he thought about just breaking into a run. That seemed to be the only solution he had lately. But something held him standing still where he was.

Dr. Sanchez walked up beside Ben. He had shaved his thick black mustache, and there were large bags under his eyes. He looked tired, Ben thought, possibly even sad.

"How are you?" Dr. Sanchez said, touching Ben's shoulder lightly. "What brings you here?"

Ben didn't answer.

"I've been reading about your races in the paper. That's really great," he said with a smile.

Ben's eyes burned into the orange and green coral shaped designs on the floor, but he didn't say a word.

"Well," Dr. Sanchez said lightly, "I…I better get back to work. It was…good to see you."

Ben wanted to nod, or at least acknowledge the man in some way, but what do you say to the man that killed your daughter?

# 7

## WATCHING HIM

The sliding glass doors closed behind Ben as he stepped outside the hospital. He closed his eyes and imagined an enclosed concrete building. On the inside there was a blue sky and several clouds, but on the outside there was nothing. He focused on the walls for several seconds, picturing himself alone inside them, away from the memories, and the noise, and the pain.

It was a method he had created to remove distractions while running that he called "creating the zone." He breathed slowly for several more seconds, and then like a wave wiping away the footprints on a beach, his mind felt clear.

Ben took several steps down the concrete walkway. About every twenty feet was a square brick planter with a large oak tree planted inside. A heavy spring breeze lifted up bunches of brown serrated oak leaves and scattered them across his feet.

To his left was a small bike rack, and just behind it a green chain link fence surrounded by several small bushes in an attempt to hide the transformer.

To his right a few concrete picnic tables. The circular kind, with out of place adornments sculpted into each base. They were all full. Two guys in scrubs sat on top of one with their feet on the bench, another was full of students in plain clothes, and at the third sat a cute blonde girl holding the remains of a sandwich in one hand, propping open a book in her other.

*You've got to be kidding me.*

\* \* \*

From a table about ten yards away, Casey Taylor finished the last of her turkey and cheese sandwich. She sat her book down and tossed a couple empty Ziplock baggies into her lunch box.

When she looked up she was surprised to see someone else sitting down at the bench on the other side of the table. She recognized him right away.

He had short dark brown hair that looked like it might be curly if he let it grow out. His features were strong and angular; he couldn't be more than a year or two older than her, if that. He was wearing blue mesh shorts that ended a couple inches above his knees and looked like they were made out of cotton as opposed to nylon. And a plain white tee-shirt with the word "Florida" written across the front in blue clung to his lean frame. His name was Benson Wilder.

"You are an extremely hard girl to find," he said.

Casey didn't respond, but instead watched as he reached across the table and grabbed her keys. "Let's try this again," he said.

"Do you have time? I mean, there are probably lots of other half-naked girls on roller blades who need to be saved."

As if on cue a group of three girls walked by. The redhead on the far side said, "Hey, Ben, good luck this weekend!"

Casey rolled her eyes, swung her lunch box over her shoulder and grabbed the keys out of his hand.

"Wait," Ben said as she stood up from the table. "Go out with me."

"What?" she said, turning around.

"Go out with me."

"I don't even know you."

"Okay, well, what would you like to know?"

She thought about it for a minute. All the boring questions popped into her mind. *Where are you from? What are you studying at UF? How do you like the track team?*

She knew the questions didn't really matter, though; in fact, she surprised herself when she realized she kind of, sort of, really did want to go out with him. She thought about Emma, though. Ultimately no twenty-something guy wanted to date a single mom. So, instead of taking a chance, she made up an excuse.

"It's my first-year residency, and I have a…" She caught herself. Only a few of her classmates knew she had a daughter, yet for some reason she almost told him.

"You have a…?"

The way he looked at her right now was so intense it was intimidating. She almost felt compelled to tell him, but she'd

27

gone down that road before and it never lead to anything good. "I have no time outside of the hospital."

The door opened behind Casey. The same door Ben had walked out a few minutes ago. A middle-aged, and somewhat overweight black woman stuck her head out, "Casey."

Casey turned around; it was Candy, one of the nurses. "Dr. Hasara is asking for you."

She looked back at Ben. "I'm sorry, I have to go."

"So, can I call you? Email? Text? Write you a letter?" Ben said as she walked away.

Casey looked back and part of her wanted all of the above, but instead she smiled, and continued walking through the sliding glass doors.

\* \* \*

"Girl, who was that fine lookin' man you was conversin' with?" Candy asked.

"Just some guy," Casey said. "Do you know what Dr. Hasara wanted?"

"Girl you need to quit changin' the subject and go look in the mirror."

Casey ran her hand through her ponytail. "Do I have something on me?"

The hallway split to the left and Dr. Hasara was standing near the nurse's desk with a clipboard in his hand. Candy kept walking straight in the other direction. Without stopping, she said, "You don't got anything on you. I just wanted you to see the look in your eyes when you talk about that boy."

Before Casey could respond, her phone buzzed in her pocket. She looked down at the screen; it was Nikki.

She didn't want to answer right now, but ever since Emma's surgery she had developed this terrible habit where she believed every phone call might be an emergency. "Nikki," she said, "is everything okay? I can't really talk right now."

"Everything will be fine if you come out with me tonight," Nikki said.

Casey didn't have any plans, and Emma was staying over at a friend's house. She was about halfway through with *Ugly Love* by Colleen Hoover and suddenly had a craving for cookie dough frozen yogurt, with chunks of brownie covered in chocolate syrup. That was all starting to sound like a good plan, so she gave the same response she always did, "I can't tonight."

Nikki didn't respond. "Nikki?" Casey said. Again no response, but this time Casey heard a sound that had become too familiar lately: crying.

"Did Trevor do something again?" Casey asked, already knowing the answer. "Are you okay?"

"Yes," Nikki managed between sobs. "I don't know."

"And how is going out tonight going to help?"

Nikki calmed down a bit. "I just…I just need to get my mind off him."

This time Casey didn't respond. To be honest she didn't really want to go out tonight, or most nights for that matter. Nikki had always been there for her though. During high school a lot of Casey's friends didn't want much to do with her after they found out she was pregnant. But Nikki was by her side through everything. That's why Casey said, "I'll meet you there around ten if you promise me one thing."

"Anything, Casey."

"Promise me it's over between you and Trevor."

"It's so over," Nikki said. "I don't want to even think about him again."

Casey looked back at Dr. Hasara who was done talking with the nurse and walking in her direction. "I really gotta go though. I'll call you when I'm off work."

# 8

## DUDE

*April 3, 2015*

Ben sat there for a few more minutes, thinking for some reason she might come running back out of the hospital. But she didn't. Apparently asking a girl out wasn't as easy as it used to be.

His phone buzzed in his pocket. He pulled it out and looked down at the screen. It was Parker.

"Hello?"

"Dude," Parker said. "Where are you? I got something awesome for us to do tonight and you can't say no."

This scenario happened about twice a week. It was kind of like Groundhog's Day, except Ben never got to do anything cool like rob an armored car, or learn ice sculpting. Still, he said the same thing he always said, "No."

And then Parker said the same thing he always said.

"I figured you might say that, but I also figured you still owe me."

"You still there?" Parker asked. Parker didn't wait for a response and instead kept talking. "Okay, I'll meet you back at the dorms around eight. We gotta leave by at least nine. Don't be late.

"Okay," Ben said.

"Dude. For real?"

"Yes, I owe you one. But if you say 'dude' one more time I'm going to reach through the phone and slap that word out of you. What is it with you guys from California and the word 'dude' anyways?"

"Dude, I don't know. Sorry, it's a habit. I'll see you back at the dorm."

# 9

## Fight Night

*April 3, 2015*

After class Ben went to heaven.

At least that's what all the football players called the Bill Heavener Athletic Complex.

The perimeter of the room was lined with offices for all the strength and conditioning coaches and nutrition specialists. While the center of the room contained just about every machine and free weight combination possible. And of course they were all specially monogrammed with the UF logo. Just in case the weights get lost. Or possibly the football players.

They didn't like it when other athletes used their facility, which is pretty much the only reason Ben worked out here: he didn't like the football players. It was late Friday afternoon though. There wasn't an athlete in the whole building that he recognized. Most of the guys in there were probably a bunch of walk-ons still trying to prove themselves, something Ben could actually relate to.

Ben put a little more into his workout than he originally planned, trying to shake his mind from the incessant thoughts about Casey Taylor.

About an hour into his workout Ashley Brannick, a six foot five, three hundred pound lineman walked into the training room. "Let's go fresh!" he yelled, referring to some of the younger guys working out.

Ben finished his last three reps on the incline bench at 225 pounds. "Holy shit," Ashley said as he walked over to Ben. "If it isn't Benson "Record Setting" Wilder. I never thought I'd see the day when one of you puny little runners would be in *my gym* puttin' up some real weight."

Ben stood up as a few of the other guys were making their way towards Ashley's beckon. He tapped Ashley on the belly as he walked by. "Some of us put up the weight," he looked back and pointed at Ashley, "and others put it on."

Ben saw a few of the guys start laughing as he walked out.

\* \* \*

By the time he got to the dorm it was a little after seven and of course the first words he heard when he walked in were…

"Dude, where the crap have you been?"

Ben tossed his backpack on his desk chair and his keys and wallet on his shelf in the closet.

"There's this thing called practice. You should ask Allen Iverson about it," Ben said.

"It was an optional Friday night workout. My guess is you and a couple student managers had some nice alone time."

Parker was right, Ben was the only runner who bothered to show up.

"Relax, it's like," Ben looked down at his watch, "It's 7:08 p.m. I don't even go out that much and even I know people aren't going out this early."

"No man, this is different. It's Fight Night," Parker said.

"What the heck is fight night?"

"I know you're only a freshman, but how the heck do you not know what fight night is. It's like the biggest night of the year. They convert the dance floor at 8 Seconds into a cage and several local MMA guys go buck wild."

Ben rolled his eyes. "Sounds amazing. Shocked I didn't know about it."

"That's not even the best part. You have to see the girls that show up at these things."

"I thought we were meeting some girls there or something."

"No, they kind of bailed…" Parker said. "It's all good, though, Brad and Jimmy's gonna meet us there."

"Brad's alright, but Jimmy?"

"Why don't we call some of your friends then? Oh that's right—everyone else on the team hates you because you're an ass."

"I'm not an ass. I'm just honest. Either way, good point."

"So, go get ready, I want to get there early and grab a table up front."

Ben walked to the bathroom and turned on the shower. "You know these girls likely come out for the ripped fighters and not the skinny runners."

"That hurts, man," Parker said.

"Maybe next time you won't skip those optional workouts."

# 10

## NIKKI

*April 3, 2015*

Casey stood in front of her bathroom mirror, adjusting the straps on her red and white polka dot chiffon blouse. Nikki walked in as she tapped the face of the black Fitbit on her left wrist. It was 8:37 p.m.

"You're not wearing *that* are you?"

Casey looked down at her shirt. "What's wrong with this shirt?"

"No. *That.*" Nikki said, pointing at her Fitbit.

"Umm, yes. I love my Fitbit." Casey double tapped the tiny horizontal screen. "Plus I still need another three thousand steps tonight," she said with a smile.

Nikki laughed and leaned forward to dab on some lipgloss with her pinky. She pursed her lips in the mirror, the soft peach matte complimenting her white strapless peplum top and black skinny jeans.

"Remind me why we're going to this thing again tonight," Casey said.

"Because there are going to be really cute guys there. And because I never get to hang out with my best friend because she always comes up with lame excuses not to go out. Did I mention the really cute guys part?"

Casey turned around and looked at her jeans in the mirror.

Nikki did the same. "I wish my butt looked that good."

Casey pointed at her Fitbit and joked, "Maybe you should consider one of these."

# 11

## Bad Idea

*April 3, 2015*

Ben looked around at the usually country-themed nightclub. The dance floor had been replaced by The Octagon: an eight sided fighting cage. It was about six feet tall with eight steel posts wrapped in thick plastic covered foam that held up vinyl coated chain-link fence panels. It looked exactly like the cage he'd seen on television, except probably ordered on Amazon and assembled by a few half-drunk college students.

Two fighters were already in the ring, and the referee was speaking to both of them about something. Instead of waitresses, there were Octagon Girls. They were wearing black, boy style, low-cut bathing suit bottoms and a matching bikini top.

It was a little past ten, which meant the first fight was slightly behind schedule. The crowd was already getting impatient and rowdy. Two fights had broken out and quickly ended by three white guys the size of John Cena. They were dragged out of the bar and their spots quickly filled by the line of students outside.

"This has got to be the worst idea ever," Ben said to himself.

"What?" Parker yelled between hundreds of shouting college students.

Ben just shook his head, "Nothing."

"This is going to be incredible!" Parker yelled. He put his arm around the girl next to him, and whispered something into her ear that made her laugh.

Her name was Nikki, short for Nicole, unless people actually name their kids Nikki. He'd met her at the bar about twenty minutes ago. She was a cute girl, and seemed nice enough, Ben thought. She also kind of seemed like every other girl though.

Ben looked across the table at one of the only empty seats left in the bar. They were apparently saving a seat for Nikki's "friend," who had been in the "bathroom" ever since Parker came back to the table with Nikki.

She leaned forward resting her elbows on the table and looked right at Ben. "You look so familiar."

Parker put his hand on Ben's shoulder. "You mean Mr. Benson Wilder?" Parker corrected himself. "The Mr. Benson Wilder, I mean."

"You're that runner," Nikki said.

Brad and Jimmy laughed from across the table.

"What's so funny?" Nikki asked.

"We're all runners," Jimmy said.

Ben leaned towards Parker. "I'm gonna grab some fresh air."

"Dude, the fight's about to start!"

39

Ben didn't respond. He just stood up, pushed in his chair and headed towards the front door.

"Okay man, we'll be here," Parker added. Nikki made eye contact with Ben as he stood up, said something to Parker and then looked back at him. Ben smiled trying to be friendly and headed back towards the entrance, feeling her eyes still locked on him.

The front of the club was even more packed than the area around the cage. As Ben looked to his right, he understood why. There was a full bar and two unbelievably hot girls behind the counter spilling more alcohol than serving it. Every guy at the bar probably thought they had a chance. Maybe somehow they'd use the right line that would end up with one of the girls writing their number down on a napkin and sliding it across the bar to them.

That was what happened in the movies, anyways. This was real life though, where the girls behind the bar were being paid to dress and act exactly how they were. Stick-on tattoos and all. Ben would bet money they'd probably rather be at home in their pajamas curled up on the couch with a good book and some ice cream. Cookie dough probably. Or maybe mint chocolate chip.

Ben looked over to the front door; the bottom line was exiting the club was starting to seem like a bad idea. There were just too many damn people standing around and the chance of him getting back in were slim to none—which actually sounded like a half-decent plan, maybe the guy version of "going to the bathroom," is "getting some fresh air."

He looked back across the room where Parker was sitting with his new girl. *I can't just leave him, though.*

Ben felt a somewhat sweaty arm wrap around his shoulders, "Well, if it isn't Mr. Track & Field himself gracing us with his presence." It was the left fielder for the baseball team, Mike Mitchel.

"So what brings Mr. Clean out tonight?" Mike said.

Mr. Clean was another nickname a lot of guys called him. It made absolutely zero sense, but whatever. For some reason athletes go around giving each other nicknames until one sticks. Hopefully this one doesn't.

"Just out with some friends tonight, man. What about you?"

Mike tilted his head towards the bar and smiled.

*Figures.*

Forced into a few minutes of small talk, Ben sighed relief when some other guy Ben didn't recognize started talking to Mike. Well, talking would be an understatement. This guy was yelling. Not in an "I want to kick your ass" way, but in an "I've already had too many drinks to realize I'm shouting at you" way.

Ben put his hand on Mike's shoulder, "I'll catch you later, man."

Mike gave him the obligatory head nod.

The commentator spoke up and the room quieted a bit, and then erupted. The fight was about to start. The two guys standing in front of him moved past him towards their seats, and Ben saw a stairwell about fifteen feet ahead of him.

A guy and a girl walked down the stairs and towards the bar. There must be roof access, he thought.

He passed three more people hurrying down the stairs as the fight bell rang. The roof was mostly empty when he reached the top of the staircase. To his right a few guys were facing the parking lot towards the back, smoking what smelled like weed. And with the intelligence level of the people in this bar, it was probably laced with something that was going to send them to the hospital shortly. About fifty feet in front of him a girl in a red shirt, jeans, and sandals was standing on the far end, looking over the railing towards the street. A guy to his left flicked a cigarette over the edge and headed towards the doorway Ben was still standing in.

Ben walked to his left and looked over the railing towards the sidewalk below. He could still see several lines of smoke puffing from the cigarette, until a passerby unknowingly stepped on it. From the roof the noises from the club were muffled, and other than the voices below on the street, it was a quiet night.

The Pepsi Invitational was tomorrow. The Tom Jones Memorial two weeks after that, and then the LSU Invitational. After that it was the SEC Championships. They were all pieces to the puzzle that once finished, were supposed to lead to the NCAA Championships. Yet as he looked out towards the streets of downtown Gainesville littered with students just trying to make tonight the best night possible, all he could think about was a girl named Casey Taylor

# 12

## CASABLANCA

*April 3, 2015*

When Casey Taylor saw Ben walk up the stairs to the roof, she immediately turned around to face the street. *You've got to be kidding me.*

Yet she smiled, the lines from *Casablanca* ringing in her head: *Of all the gin joints, in all the towns, in all the world, you had to walk into mine....* She was a sucker for old movies. Probably because several years ago she found out when you're pregnant, hungry, and wide awake at two in the morning, there isn't much else to do.

Moving as little as possible, she held up her phone and reversed the camera like she was taking a selfie. It was dark, and at first she couldn't see anything. She angled it up towards the light to refocus and then to the right where a group of guys were still passing around a joint and laughing. She angled it the other way, but again nothing. She panned back to the stairwell that was almost directly behind her and nearly dropped the phone. He was walking directly towards her.

Casey clicked the lock screen button and dropped her phone back into her purse. She was suddenly glad she wore jeans. She felt almost exposed as he approached her. At the last minute she turned around, not sure what else to do. She thought maybe she should apologize about lying earlier. Although, it really was true, she didn't have a lot of time for anything outside the hospital.

As she turned around there was only one problem. The guy walking towards her, who was now about five feet from her, wasn't Ben. She didn't recognize the guy. Just some random guy from the bar.

From the corner of her eye, Casey saw something move. She looked to her right and Ben turned around, leaning his back against the fence. When their eyes met, he grinned. It was an annoying grin. It was a when-you're-done-with-that-loser-you-can-come-talk-to-me-but-for-now-I'll-just-watch grin.

*If he wants to play that way, then maybe I will talk to this loser.*

"I think it's time I tell you what people are saying behind your back," the guy said.

"What?" Casey said, confused.

"Nice ass."

"What did you just say?"

"You know, the…the thing they say behind your back…" the guy stuttered, almost shocked this pick up line didn't work.

The guy's eyes kept wandering all over her body and she realized talking to this guy isn't worth wiping the grin off Ben's face. She stepped closer and very quietly spoke. "I think it's time I tell you what people are saying behind your back."

"What's that?" he said, excitedly.

"You got maced on the roof of 8 Seconds by a girl." Casey reached towards her purse.

"Whoa, okay, okay. Damn girl." He held up his hands again and backed away. "You don't gotta go all Ronda Rousey on me."

*This is why I don't go out,* she thought.

Casey looked over to where Ben was standing, but he wasn't standing there anymore. Instead, he was sitting with his legs hanging over the side of the building and his arms slumped over the mid-rail. Something about the way he sat there looked almost…sad, she thought.

She was already moving towards him before she could think of a reason not to. The brick wall was cool, but rough through her jeans as she sat down next to him and scooted up to the railing. She sat her purse in between them to act as a small barrier. He looked at her with the same intensity as before.

His lips started to subtly curl as he spoke. "I think it's time I tell you what people are saying behind your back."

Casey rolled her eyes. "I'm so glad one of us enjoyed that."

"Hey, you gotta give the guy a little bit of credit. Most guys can't even get up the courage to say anything. And when they do, they just get some lame excuse only to see the girl out later that night, completely shattering their confidence and preventing them from ever asking a girl out again. It's how all the good girls end up with bad guys."

"That's not true," she said. But the moment the words left her mouth she wondered if it was. She didn't feel good about the earlier exchange anymore, and didn't know what else to say, which led to Ben being quiet again.

The streets below them were full of trash and beer bottles. Students were making their way from bar to bar, mostly in gender divided groups. Ben was right, most of the guys wouldn't even approach the girls. Occasionally some idiot would cat call or say something stupid to a group of girls as they passed. *Why on earth do guys ever think that's going to work?*

She tried to look over at Ben without actually moving, so he wouldn't notice. *I wonder what he's thinking. Is he wondering what I'm thinking, or is he thinking about something else entirely?* Then an idea popped into her head. *Why don't I just ask him? Technically he told me earlier I could ask him anything.* So she did. "What are you thinking?"

"Do you *really* want to know? Or is this just one of those questions that are supposed to break the awkward silence."

"I actually like the silence," she said. "But…I really want to know."

"Are you sure? Because thoughts aren't like words. They don't always make sense."

"I want to know."

"Okay, well. I was thinking about how I dislike when people are mean to dogs." Ben paused for a moment and then he continued. "And what practice would be like next week; Coach always likes to change things up. And about what type of person you are and if those sandals are any indication. And lastly, about how I love chocolate pecan pie, especially when my sister makes it for Thanksgiving."

That was a lot more than she ever expected him to say. She looked down at her black Steve Madden sandals. Her jeans stopped just short of the gladiator style leather straps that ran over the top of her foot and a few inches of her heel.

It's not like they were slutty stilettos. "What's wrong with my sandals?" *I love these sandals.*

He laughed. "Nothing, I like your sandals. They are very chill."

Casey raised her eyebrows slightly. "Chill?"

"Yeah, like you look relaxed, instead of strutting around in three inch heels like a lost chicken."

Casey laughed quietly. She imagined all the girls in the club walking kind of funny and bobbing their heads as they moved. "I could absolutely go for some pecan pie right now too."

"I know, right?"

"Yo, Ben!" someone yelled as they ran onto the balcony. Ben turned around; it was Mike Mitchel again.

"What's up, Mike?"

"Your boy Parsley is about to get his ass beat."

"Parsley?" Ben asked, confused.

"I don't know his fuckin' name man. It's your boy."

"Parker?"

"Yeah, whatever. He's about to get his face kicked in."

# 13

## Black and Blue

*April 3, 2015*

Casey ran after Ben, who was running after Mike. She fell behind as he took the stairs two and three at a time.

*I'm so wearing sneakers next time I go out.*

She reached the bottom of the stairs just in time to see Ben follow Mike out the back exit. The crowd was hyped up and rowdy after the first fight. She bumped into several people as she zigzagged her way through the tables. She had almost made it to the back door when the last table must have gotten word of the fight outside. A tall sandy-blond guy with a pink and white plaid shirt stood up from the table the same time she tried to pass and Casey ran straight into the side of him.

Unfortunately he was holding a full cup of beer, which had now been emptied onto the girl that was sitting to his right.

Casey looked down at the girl. "I'm so sorry," she said.

"You little bitch," the girl replied.

The guy she bumped into was trying not to laugh, but he couldn't help it. "Have fun with this one tonight," Casey said. She quickly made her way outside before anything else happened.

When she stepped through the back door she could see a crowd of people already forming around the guys she guessed were Parker and some frat guy. This wasn't one of those khaki shorts, boat shoes, and sweater-vest frat guys. This was one of those crazy, drunk, and obsessed with shooting-himself-in-the-butt-with-steroids frat guys. This was Nikki's ex, Trevor.

Casey looked back at Parker. He was actually pretty tall, probably a couple inches over six feet. Unfortunately he was about 150 pounds dripping wet and looked like he probably knew more about badminton than fighting.

Casey couldn't make out what anyone was saying because they were all screaming something different. Though she was pretty sure the people crowding around only cared about one thing: a fight.

That's when she saw Ben step in front of Parker.

\* \* \*

Inserting himself between the two, Ben held up his hands like he was trying to stop a truck. The big guy took a step back with his right leg, and Ben stopped. "Whoa, man. Why don't we take this back inside and talk. I'm sure it was just some misunderstanding. I can buy you," Ben motioned behind the guy, "and your boys a drink."

The guy looked back at his buddies, unsure what to do. Most of them looked like a free drink sounded like a good idea. But there's always that one window licker that has to ruin it for everyone else. "He hit on your girl, Trevor," the guy yelled. "You let that go and next thing you know he'll be hitting on your mom."

Ben glared back at Parker, and then over to Nikki standing behind him.

Ben heard another group of people mumbling several things to the right of him. "Isn't that Benson Wilder?" one guy said.

"The runner?" another guy asked.

"Yeah."

"Yeah, I think it is."

At the same time Mike and a few of his boys walked over behind Ben. He recognized one that played on the baseball team with Mike, but he didn't recognize the other three.

Mike spoke loud enough for everyone to hear. "You alright, Ben?"

The words distracted Trevor for a second.

"Yeah, I believe Trevor," Ben said motioning towards the big guy standing across from him, "was just heading back inside."

The same chucklehead from before yelled again, "Beat his ass, Trevor!" And then another one, "Stomp his ass, man." Ben looked back over at the group of guys behind Trevor and realized he was wrong. Trevor wouldn't be going inside anytime soon, which meant it was time for Plan B.

"Aren't you a little worried that your boys seem to be somewhat preoccupied with another guy's ass?" The guy looked behind him towards friends, momentarily confused, and then turned back to Ben and clinched his fist. "Move out of the fucking way."

Ben looked down and sighed. He stepped to the left to give the guy a clear path to Parker. Then he said, "I'm sorry."

The guy looked confused again. Why was he apologizing? The confused look never left his face as Ben reared back and kicked him right between the legs. The guy fell forward to the ground, but before Ben knew what was happening a blur entered his vision from just behind him and to the right. His head snapped to the left as he brought his hand up to his right eye that was now stinging.

Some little shit just blind-sided him. The kid was winding up again, and then he was down on the ground. Parker had just kicked him between the legs too.

Several people in the crowd started laughing, and then Mike and his boys jumped in along with several of the other frat guys. Ben took two steps towards the fray, but suddenly Casey was pulling Ben towards the street, with Nikki following.

Casey looked in Nikki's direction when they got to the street. "I thought you and Trevor were done?"

Nikki looked at her like, *not now.*

"You okay?" Casey said.

"Yeah," Nikki said. "We can talk about it later."

Ben looked back to find Parker and saw him stuck between the two groups of guys. Then Parker darted back inside the club. Ben was about to run back in when Casey pulled him again towards her car that was parked across the street. Parker, you are on your own now, Ben thought.

Casey was laughing when they got in the car.

Ben was still touching his hand to his eye. "I'm glad one of us enjoyed that."

"Guys, uh, maybe we should go," Nikki said pointing at Trevor and the guy Parker kicked running towards the car.

She pulled away from the curb, nearly swiping the tailgate of the truck in front of her, and turned west down University Avenue. "Did you really tell that guy a joke before you kicked him in the balls?"

"It was either that or run in like an idiot, which Parker already seemed to have covered." Ben looked back at Nikki. "What the heck happened anyways?"

"I didn't know he was going to be there," Nikki said.

"You didn't know who was going to be there?" Ben asked.

"Trevor," Casey said. She looked at Nikki through the rear-view mirror. "Who is *supposed* to be her ex."

"He *is* my ex," Nikki said.

Ben looked back at Nikki again. "But how did Parker and Trevor end up outside?"

"When you left I guess Trevor saw me with Parker. He came over, and at first was just talking to me, apologizing and everything. I asked him to leave and he wouldn't. Next thing I know Parker is standing asking him to leave. Trevor's stupid friends came over, and I don't know."

Casey interrupted the conversation. "Where are you parked?"

"I'm not. I rode with Jen, but she didn't stay. Actually I just texted her, and she's over at Gator City if you guys want to go?"

"I think I've had enough fun for the night," Casey said.

"Will you drop me off? It's just up here on the right."

A few blocks ahead Casey stopped at the light and Nikki got out. She leaned down against the car where Ben's window was open. "Take care of my girl," she said with a wink.

*Nikki!* Casey mouthed.

"Will do," Ben said, winking back at her.

Nikki walked towards the back patio of Gator City as the light turned green.

"You think that was a good idea?" Ben asked as they drove away.

"As opposed to?"

"I don't know, maybe…not leaving her right now."

"She's a big girl, Mr. Sensitive. Besides Jen is there."

Casey looked over to Ben and swerved a few feet into the oncoming lane. "Now let me see your eye."

"How about you just focus on the road."

"Don't be such a baby. Now turn this way so I can see it."

Ben turned his head all the way to the left, so she could see his right eye.

"Good news is, you're not going to die. Bad news is your jokes are terrible," she said, laughing.

# 14

## First Date

April 3, 2015

Five minutes later Casey was following Ben into his dorm room, after insisting on taking a quick look at his eye.

Ben sat his keys down on the desk that was immediately to the left of the door, and Casey's eyes scanned over the rest of the room.

There was a closet next to the desk that had no doors revealing several shirts on hangers and about ten pairs of sneakers on the floor below them. Another desk sat directly across the room and acted like a dividing line between the two beds. Above the bed on the right was a post of Megan Fox bending over a motorcycle, another post of three well-endowed blondes in white bikinis, and a close up of Emma Stone's gorgeous green eyes.

Ben sat down on the other bed. The walls above it were empty except for a paper sized photo of a guy running and a quote she couldn't make out.

She walked over to the mini fridge next to his bed. "Seriously? All you have are frozen chicken patties and some Cheetos? I thought athletes were supposed to be healthy? And why are the Cheetos in the 'fridge?

"Did you think I'd have a fridge full of fruits, vegetables, and vitamins? And because everything stays fresher in the 'fridge.

"Actually, yeah. And that's dumb." She grabbed the bag of frozen chicken patties and turned around to the bed where he was sitting. "Put this on your face." Ben took the frozen bag and pressed it up against his eye. He leaned back so he was half sitting up, half leaning on right arm. "Tell me something about you," he said.

"What?"

"Well, we can't just sit here in silence, so tell me something about you."

"How about *you* tell *me* something about *you*?"

"How about we go back and forth?"

Casey thought about it for a moment, and then sat down on the bed next to him. "Deal."

"I'll go first," Ben said. "I like fried chicken and Cheetos." He laughed, but it hurt, and in between each attempt he grimaced.

"Seriously, your jokes are soooo bad," she said, trying not to smile. She thought about something she could tell Ben, but only dumb things came to mind, like her favorite color. And Emma of course, but she definitely wasn't going there.

"Well?" he said.

"I don't know."

"Alright, well the rules clearly stipulate that you now have to answer any four questions of my choosing."

"That's what the rules say, huh?"

"Yep, very specific. Page 23, subparagraph A. I would show you, but unfortunately I let someone borrow my only copy."

She was a little nervous what he might ask. "I guess I'll have to take your word for it then."

Ben got up, still holding the frozen patties to his face and grabbed a pencil and notepad. He sat back on the bed and put the frozen patties down next to him. "Okay if I take these off for a minute?"

"Yeah, but you need to put them back on in about ten minutes."

"Okay, question number one…"

"Wait you're going to write down my answers?" Casey asked.

"You'll see. Okay, question number one. You walk into your house, and everything is white. The wall, the ceiling, the floor, everything. What do you feel the moment you step through the door?"

"And everything is white?" Casey said.

"Yep. White as white can be."

"Okay, I guess I probably feel peaceful, but also somewhat alone."

"Question two. What feeling do you get when you see your favorite color?"

Casey thought about it. Her favorite color was red. "I guess I feel alive and passionate."

"Question number three. Describe the qualities of your favorite animal."

"That's technically not a question," Casey pointed out. "But, I would have to say…"

"No, no, let me rephrase. What are the qualities of your favorite animal?"

"Like I was saying…loyal, and kind, and wise in that quiet way, because I love dogs."

Ben made an audible noise as he wrote down her answer. "Hmmm."

"What? Is that bad?"

"Okay, last question. Imagine yourself near a large body of water. What do you do?"

"Well, if it's a nice day I'd see if the water was cool, and as long as it wasn't too cold I'd jump in and go for a swim."

Ben finished writing, put the frozen bag back on his face and held out the notebook. "Now, normally I charge for this, but tonight I'll make an exception."

She grabbed the notebook out of his hands and looked down at what he had written.

*1. You perceive death to be…peaceful, but lonely.*

*2. You see yourself as a person who is…alive and passionate.*

*3. People see you as…loyal, kind, and wise.*

*4. When you fall in love you…are hesitant at first and then dive in.*

Casey read what he had written twice. She knew it was just a game, but the statements felt so full of truth, especially the one about love. "Where did you learn to do that?"

"Just something I used to do with…just something I used to do," he corrected.

Ben sat up and lifted the frozen bag off his face and looked at Casey.

"Can I ask you one last question?"

Before Casey could respond, Ben asked anyways. "Where would you like to go on our second date?"

Casey looked up at him with a lips closed smile. "Remind me when our first date was again?"

"Well tonight, of course."

Casey laughed. "This is your idea of a date?"

"No, but you can't deny it's the quintessential college town date."

"How do you figure?"

"Well, we went to a nightclub…"

"Technically, we were inside together for less than a minute," Casey interrupted.

"I walked you home."

"You mean, *I drove you* home."

"You invited me inside."

Casey didn't bother correcting him, she just rolled her eyes this time.

"And then you kissed me goodnight."

Casey started to speak, but Ben leaned in and kissed her. The right side of his lips where the frozen pack had been, were cold, while the left side was soft and warm. He held his lips against hers for a moment, and the dichotomy of the two temperatures felt invigorating.

Then he pulled away slowly. "Sorry, I mean, then *I* kissed *you*. If we're back to being all technical about things."

It had been so long since she'd been kissed, that it felt like a first kiss all over again. She just sat there for a moment, looking back at him, and thinking about the kiss. And at the same time trying not to think about the kiss.

The sound of her phone interrupted them. For a moment she thought about ignoring it. She wanted him to kiss her again the exact same way.

The second ring snapped her back to that same bad habit. She got up and rifled through her purse that was sitting on his desk.

She looked down at the lit up screen and the answered. "Bianca, is everything alright? Okay, I'll be over in a few minutes." She hung up the phone.

Ben stood up. "Is everything okay?"

"Yes, I just have to go."

"Do you want me to go with you? Or is there something I can do?"

"No, no, it's nothing like that. I just forgot about something," she lied.

Ben moved towards the door as Casey dropped her phone back in her purse and pulled out her keys.

Ben smiled, grimacing a little again. "If it's not an emergency, then I can't let you leave without at least giving me your number."

She looked up at him and it was the first time she realized how tall he was compared to her. He wasn't tall and lanky, though, like Parker. His frame was still lean, but more like a baseball player, or a surfer.

She walked back over to his desk, grabbed a pen and one of the yellow sticky tabs. She wrote down her number and then folded the paper in half. He stepped out of the way as she handed it to him.

"I had fun tonight," he said as she walked out.

"Me too."

A few steps from her car and Casey's phone rang again. "Bianca, I'm on my way. What? Are you sure? Okay."

False alarm. It wasn't Emma who threw up, it was one of the other girls at the sleepover.

Casey stood in front of her car, looking down at her phone, and then back up to the window of Ben's dorm room. The light was on, but the curtains were closed, so she couldn't see anything else. She thought about walking back up to his room. She thought about that kiss again. But her phone rang again.

She looked back down. It was Nikki.

"Hey, are you okay?" Casey said.

"I'm fine. Trevor showed up at Gator City, so I just left before he could start anything else."

"That's probably a good idea," Casey said. "Wait, how did you leave? I thought you rode with Jen?"

"I did, but she's staying over at her boyfriend's tonight, so she said I could take the car. I'm actually only a few minutes from your house, do you mind if I crash with you tonight?"

"I'm not home…" Casey said.

"Wait, where are you?" Nikki answered her own question. "Oh my gosh, are you still with Benson Wilder?"

"Why are you saying his full name like that? And no, I just left."

"Uh, because he's Benson Wilder."

"How do you even know his full name?"

"He was on ESPN for breaking some old running record last month. And then they did a feature of him in the Alligator."

"He kissed me," Casey blurted out, feeling a smile slowly form as she opened the door to her car.

"Okay, I'm turning around to pick up Pokey Stix and pizza from Gumby's and you're going to tell me all the details when I get there."

Even though it was only a little past eleven, Casey was tired, but a wave of energy shot through her body as she thought about Ben, and she had to admit she was a little excited to tell Nikki all the details about their first kiss.

# 15

## KISS AND TELL

*April 3, 2015*

Nikki put the pizza and cheese bread on the coffee table in front of the couch and sat down.

A few seconds later Casey walked out of her bedroom in white sweatpants and a gray "Trust me I'm a doctor" tee shirt that Nikki bought her when she arrived in Gainesville last year. She pulled the rubber band off her wrist and pulled her hair back into a ponytail as she sat down.

Casey looked over at Nikki who was staring at her. "What?"

"Do you know you haven't stopped smiling since you got home?"

Casey hadn't really thought about it. She'd been too busy still thinking about Ben.

"Wash your face…smiling. Change your clothes…smiling. Sitting on the couch…smiling."

Casey moved her hands up to her lips. Her mouth was open and her lips were slightly curled. She was smiling…

"So what was it like?" Nikki said.

"The kiss?"

Nikki tilted her head to the side. "Yes the kiss!"

"It was…" Casey started. "It was…like that feeling you get when you're cold, and then you step out into the sun and a tingling warmth spreads across your entire body."

Nikki looked down at her arms. "You seriously just gave me the chills."

"There's something else," Casey said.

Nikki's eyes lit up.

"Tonight wasn't the first time I met Benson Wilder."

# 16

## Joke

*April 4, 2015*

"Is this some type of fucking joke to you guys?" Coach Melvick paced the locker room. Ben, Parker, and Brad had been standing against their lockers for the last few minutes, waiting for Coach to blow a gasket.

"We're five points behind going into the 5000, with a depth of scoring of eight. Do you imbeciles have any idea what that even means?"

A depth of scoring of eight meant the top eight runners of each heat could score points for their team. Ben had thought about being a smartass and answering, but luckily Coach didn't give him time.

"I have neither the time nor the crayons to explain this to you. At least one of you need to place in the top three while also managing to prevent Georgia from reaching the top eight.

Coach waved his hand in Ben's direction, then towards Parker and Brad. "I've got one idiot with a black eye, another with a bruised leg, and a third that nearly gets lost every day on his way to practice."

Ben rubbed the dark blue bruising just below his eye, while Parker continued rubbing out his leg.

"So, I'm going to keep this simple," Coach said. "Get out of my locker room and win the damn race."

Brad was the first through the door, followed by Parker. Coach grabbed Ben by the shoulder as he walked by. For a moment he just stared Ben straight in the eyes. "Remember what started all of this."

Ben simply nodded, knowing Coach was talking about a lot more than what happened at the bar last night.

# 17

## Letting Go

*April 6, 2015*

"Dude, you've got to let it go," Parker said as him and Ben stepped off the sidewalk and onto Stadium Road. They passed The Hub on their left, along with about 200 students standing in line at Chick-fil-a.

Two cute girls walked by. "Congrats on the win, Ben," they said in unison.

"Thanks," Parker said. "My race went well too. Geez, it's like I'm not even alive. I know you got first and all, but did no one see me cut that guy from Georgia off for eighth? I mean that was the freaking clincher!"

"If it makes you feel any better, *I* think you had a nice race."

"I don't get it though, you have girls falling all over the place for you and you're caught up with some girl you hardly know. I thought you were like giving up girls or something, and now you're obsessed over this one."

"Wait, what? When did I say I was giving up girls?"

"I don't know, man. You're given this second chance at life basically, a full ride to one of the most prominent college athletic departments in the country, where you miraculously turn into this star athlete, and it's taken me nearly a year to even get you out of the damn dorm room."

"So, when exactly did I say this again?"

"Well, I guess, you didn't. But with everything that happened…"

"One, I told you not to ever go there. And two, I don't know what the deal is with this girl." Ben paused. "I just…I don't know."

They walked on the pebble sidewalk between the Liberal Arts and Computer Science building that opened up to a small courtyard. A group of students had duct taped a makeshift dance floor to the ground and were break dancing. Some students stopped and watched, or even joined in, but Ben and Parker kept walking.

"Okay, well if you like her this much, then fill in some blanks for me. You met her at Fight Night, you take her back to your place, and you don't even get a number?"

"Not exactly," Ben said.

"Well, what exactly?" Parker said.

The huge iron bell in Century Tower interrupted them and they took a right on Newell Drive and then a left towards Little Hall. They passed a couple guys from the football team and Ben gave the obligatory head nod, then answered Parker's question. "She gave me her number."

Parker stopped. "Wait a minute, if this girl gave you her number, then why the heck don't you just call her."

"Thanks, genius, that was insightful."

"No problem," Parker smirked. "But seriously."

"I called her Saturday before the race."

"And?"

"And she didn't answer or call back."

"Okay, so call her again."

"I called her Sunday, and the same thing."

Parker was about to speak, but Ben interrupted him. "And I called her again yesterday and left a message. No call back, nothing."

"Okay, well, call her again. I mean, you pretty much have two options. Keep calling until she answers, or give up."

Ben conveniently left out the fact that he had texted her this morning with no response.

Parker slapped Ben on the shoulder. "How 'bout this, there's no meet this weekend, we can go out Thursday or Friday and find you another girl. We'll call it Mission Benpossible."

Ben laughed and looked over at Parker. "I appreciate it, but I think I'll pass."

"Alright, well, catch me after class. I'll be at Broward Dining."

Ben hiked his backpack up on his shoulder. "Alright."

"And don't spend all class thinking about that girl."

Ben started walking east towards class. The problem was now beyond just thinking about it. It was knowing how good it felt just to be near her.

# 18

## Emergency

*April 6, 2015*

"You sure you don't mind picking up Emma from school?" Casey said. It was her day off, but the hospital just called, and the queasiness from avoiding the first rings made her too sick to *not* answer. "It should only be a few hours, so I should be back by dinner."

"Casey. Why do you do this every time?" Nikki said.

Casey shrugged as she pulled her hair up into a ponytail. "I don't know. I just, don't like imposing, I guess."

"It's not imposing. I would tell you if it was. Honestly, if you had another room, I'd be begging you to let me move in."

"Okay," Casey said. "If I'm not back by 6 p.m., then there is lasagna left over for you and Emma." She grabbed her phone, and swiped her finger across the home screen. A missed call still showed because she still hadn't cleared the missed call from Ben yesterday. But now she also had an unread text. Casey stared at the screen for a second, reading his name: *Benson*

*Wilder.* Before she could put her phone back in her purse, Nikki snatched it away from her.

Nikki read the text aloud. "Still waiting for that second date. Casey. Anisc. Taylor," Nikki said in a motherly tone. "You've got to be kidding me. Ben has called you…" Nikki scrolled through the calls, "…three times! And texted you. And you haven't called him back?"

"I don't know," Casey said. "I mean, what's the point?"

"What's the point? Did you not get a good look at him? His eyes, his arms, his hair. And don't even get me started on his legs in those running shorts."

"I just need to focus on other things right now," Casey said.

"Please tell me you're not holding back because of Emma."

"I'm not," Casey lied.

Nikki put her hand on her hip and raised her eyebrows.

"I promise," Casey lied again.

"I swear you must be the only girl I know who doesn't want to have a fling with a college athlete."

Casey grabbed her phone and headed for the door. She turned around towards Nikki, still standing by the kitchen table. "I don't want a fling," she said.

"Then what do you want?"

"I don't know," she said as she stepped out the door. But she did know, even after just one night with him. She wanted more.

# 19

## NOT READY

It was a few minutes after five o'clock when Casey walked past a nurse's desk painted to look like a child snorkeling with Manatees. She had just spoken with the attending physician, who confirmed she could head out for the night. When she stepped outside the frigid hospital she could feel the heat of the sun like it were hanging just above the trees, but there was nothing but scattered shadows at the bottom of the steps where Candy was sitting.

"Girl, you got problems," Candy said, picking up their conversation where they had left off about an hour ago. Candy was pretty much the only person besides Nikki that Casey felt comfortable talking to. She was about twenty years older than Casey, which made for a great friendship because she had such a drastically different perspective on life.

Casey leaned against the railing a step below her. "You sound just like Nikki."

"I don't know Miss Nikki, but she sounds like an intelligent lady."

"She is…I think," Casey said, laughing.

"And yet you still look confused."

"I just don't know what to do," Casey said.

The door opened behind her and one of fourth-year residents walked outside, eyes glued to the phone in his hands.

"I'm starting to think this whole doctor school thing didn't really teach you all that much," Candy said.

"So, I should call him back? What if he knows I've been ignoring his calls? What do I even say?"

"You hand Miss Candy the phone and I'll take care of all that," Candy said, with a smile.

*I wish I had her confidence,* Casey thought. "What if I'm not ready? I haven't even gone on a real date since I left California."

"Were you ready for him to kiss you?"

"Well, no."

"But you liked it?"

Casey blushed lightly, "Yes."

Candy pursed her bright pink lips. "Okay, okay, I get it. But there's something else."

Candy was pointing at Casey and bouncing her hand up and down like she was ringing up someone on a cash register. "Oh, no. I know that look. This is where you explain some crazy white girl stuff you into. Like you own a baby alligator or something."

Casey hadn't laughed this hard in a long time. Wait no, that's not true. This is about how hard she laughed last week at lunch when she caught Candy teaching a room full of residents how to twerk. And it wasn't just the female residents.

Casey ran her fingers over the rough surface of the railing where several paint chips were peeling off. She thought about Emma and her expression changed to a more serious one. Casey took a deep breath. "I have a daughter."

All of her classmates at UC Berkeley had known about Emma. They were surprisingly supportive, especially after the surgery. But when Casey got to Shands last summer, everything just felt different. She didn't have the comfort of her tight-knit group of med students. So, other than Nikki, her attending, and the chief resident, Candy was the first person she'd told.

"Wait, you a baby momma?" Candy looked Casey up and down. "With that body?" She took a sip of her peach tea. "I need to start that Weight Watchers again. Mhmm."

Casey laughed again. She was so glad she had met Candy in the past couple months. It was so easy talking to her.

"What's her name?" Candy asked.

"Emma Mae," Casey said. "She just turned five."

"Now *that* is a precious name."

Casey pulled the small black neck wallet from under her scrubs. The pocket was large enough for a little bit of cash, a credit card, her hospital ID, and a picture of Emma. "This is her," she said, handing the picture to Candy.

In the picture Emma was leaning against their new house in Gainesville. Her long brown hair had a slightly auburn tint and was half pulled back with lightly twisted bangs. Her lips were pouty and the color of fresh cranberries.

Candy held the picture arm's length away from her so she could see Casey next to Emma. "She's got her momma's look.

73

But those eyes…" Candy's voice trailed off. Casey knew exactly what she was seeing because she had seen it so many times herself since the surgery. Unlike her Cerulean blue eyes, Emma's were a rare mixture of stark blue and subtle green aquamarine, like the color of the ocean along the coast.

Candy handed the picture back to Casey. "She is just beautiful."

"She is. But, you understand now?"

"Understand what?"

"Why I don't think I can go out with him."

"The only reason you can't go out with him is because you left it up to Siri to call him back instead of doing it yourself."

Casey shook her head. "You don't understand, it's just not that easy."

"Girl, don't you be givin' me this single mama stuff now. I got two little girls of my own with no daddy, and while I am very protective of who is around them, I don't let that stop me from finding my soulmate."

"I just don't think I can, though."

"Look at me." Casey looked up to find Candy's hard brown eyes drilling into hers. "No one thinks they can, until they do."

"What if he finds out about Emma and doesn't like her. Or doesn't like me because I have her…" Casey said.

"First off, he's not going to *find out* about her because you're going to *tell him* about her. Secondly, if he doesn't like you because you have a little girl, then you don't want him anyways. That is not a man. That is a boy. And you don't have time for boys."

*She's right,* Casey thought. I can't go through life thinking like this. "So, what do I do now?"

# 20

## PATIENCE

*April 6, 2015*

"Any bright ideas?" Ben said.

Parker looked up from several sheets of paper spread out across the table. He was rubbing his hands over his eyes.

"About?"

"Finding Casey…," Ben said.

"I don't know, man, but I think my eyeballs are going to actually fall out of my head. This whole school thing makes zero sense. Think about it, if a single teacher can't teach us every subject, then how can they expect us to learn them all?"

Ben thought about it, and actually, it was a decent point.

"Luckily they got brownies today, man, or I honestly wouldn't still be here." Parker scarfed down his third brownie and chased it with a glass of milk.

Ben just watched as more brownie crumbs joined several that were already scattered across the papers and his lap. He couldn't even drink the milk without several drops running down the glass and onto his shirt.

"What?" Parker said, looking up at Ben staring at him.

Ben just shook his head. "Nothin', man."

"You know, if you would have just gotten Nikki's number like a normal guy then we wouldn't have this problem," Ben said

Parker looked at Ben confused.

"Because you could call Nikki and find out why Casey isn't calling me back…"

"Oh, well some warning before you decked the guy and ran would have been nice."

"I didn't run…I got pulled away by Casey."

"Whatever, man, why are you still even talking about this? I thought we agreed on Mission Benpossible."

"Sometimes I wonder if you ever listen to the words that come out of my mouth."

Parker looked over to the pizza bar where the chef had just placed a fresh tray of something. "I'm gonna grab some food, you want anything?"

Ben didn't bother responding because Parker was already walking away. He just sat there, still staring at the pile of papers that Parker called notes. He thought about going to the hospital again, but that wasn't exactly a surefire solution. He could sit outside the hospital, perhaps even around lunch time at the same bench, but there were so many problems with that. For starters, he knew it was likely she didn't get a lunch break at the same time every day. Second, the chance that she was still even at the Children's Hospital was slim, since she was a first-year resident, and they probably got transferred all over the place. And lastly there would be no guarantee she would even be working whichever day he sat there.

Parker walked back up to the table with a plate full of pizza. "Dude, you need to try some of this."

It looked absolutely disgusting. "What the heck is that?"

"Breakfast pizza," Parker said with a mouth full of pizza and a grin. "Eggs, bacon, onions, cheddar cheese, salsa, and pizza."

"It's not even breakfast time though."

"It's like a fluffy bite of heaven," Parker said between bites.

"You have problems."

Parker looked down at the scattered mess of papers in front of him. "Don't even get me started on problems." He took another bite of that disgusting pizza and then asked, "So what are you going to do now?"

"I don't…"

Parker interrupted, "Why don't you just go to the hospital again?"

"I thought about that. The chances of that working are about as good as you passing this chem test," he said, pointing back to sheets of paper spilling from a notebook in front of him.

Parker swallowed another bite of pizza and looked at Ben. "Dude, look around you. There are like twenty hot girls in this room alone. I don't know how many times I can keep saying this. We can go talk to each and every one of them right now and I guarantee you'll get at least one number." He paused and then winked, "A real number this time."

Ben stared blankly at him.

"You know, because she probably gave you a fake number."

"Yes, I got the joke dumbass. But I also got her voicemail. It's her number."

Parker took another bite of pizza. "Seriously, look around you."

Ben did look around him. There were two unbelievable blondes sitting in a booth together. Both of them wearing teal shirts with the sorority insignia for Delta Gamma, or "dirty girls" as Parker referred to them. A few tables away from them was a beautiful brunette sitting with two guys. Ben turned back the other way, and across from them was a cute red head sitting alone, doing what looked like a crossword puzzle.

The truth was Parker was right. Ben pulled his backpack on and pushed his stool in at the high-top table.

"Where are you going?" Parker asked.

Ben stood up from the table, "I don't know man. Need to clear my head."

"And what about the girl?"

Ben looked back at Parker, but didn't say anything. Instead he walked out of the cafeteria with more than one girl on his mind.

\* \* \*

Ben tried to focus on his breathing pattern as he moved across the empty track. He inhaled through his nose for three steps. *Nnihhhhh.* And exhaled through his mouth for two steps. *Sshhhhhoooo.* He picked up the pace changing his pattern to a two-one: breathing in for two steps, and out for one. His body temperature rising with each stride until he could feel the sweat on his skin evaporate trying to cool him down.

But no matter how hard he tried to focus, the silence of the vacant track began to crowd in on his thoughts. Parker's words resonated within him. *What about the girl?*

He stopped running in front of the east bleachers, bent over and rested his hands on his knees. His chest and back rose and fell as his lungs expanded and contracted to pull in more oxygen.

The fence across from him rattled from the wind and Ben looked up. The wind pushed the gate open until it clanged against the fence, and for a moment he saw her just as he first saw her six years ago…

Ben was a senior in high school and she was a new transfer whose name he didn't even know. She was tall and slender with long brunette hair that curled just slightly at the ends. Her lips were full and there were subtle dimple like creases at the edges of her mouth when she smiled.

It was only by pure chance that she was meeting a friend at the track that day. Ben didn't believe in love at first sight, but he could still remember the moment when their eyes met. It was in that moment he knew this girl mattered to him. And he hadn't had another moment like that until he met Casey Taylor.

He closed his eyes and she was gone once again. It had been five years since he lost Amanda. He could be patient.

# 21

## Risk Everything

*April 9, 2015*

A few days later, Casey made her way through campus for the first time since her orientation at the beginning of the year. As a resident, there weren't many reasons for her to be on campus outside of the hospital.

It was unbelievably crowded for a Thursday afternoon. But she'd been the type of student who scheduled her classes at seven or eight in the morning, so what did she know? Maybe this was a typical Thursday afternoon.

She could have taken the bus. It went literally everywhere on campus, even a stop just in front of the track. But for some reason she'd convinced herself walking would give her more time to think.

She took a left off the crowded sidewalk and cut across the north lawn just in front of Reitz Union.

Most of the campus was to the east of her, and she was now walking west. So, the farther she walked, the less crowded it got, until she was finally walking by herself.

She passed by Ben Hill Griffith Stadium on her right, where the football team played. Then the O'Connell Center, where the basketball team played. A few minutes later she walked by the blue-screened outfield fence of McKethan Stadium, where the baseball team played. Nikki had dragged her to all these places the second she arrived at UF. All the games were fun the first time, but it wasn't the same as undergrad at California.

Casey stopped in front of a huge stadium sign that read "James G. Pressly Stadium." The name reminded her of that one actress, Jamie Pressly. She took a step forward to read the smaller print and a guy jogged past her, clipping her purse, the contents of which spilled all over the sidewalk.

"Sorry!" the guy yelled over his shoulder. She bent down to pick everything up. She grabbed the keys attached to her UF ID, wiping the latter against her pants, the same way Ben had the first time they met.

The wind gusted and a rectangular aluminum sign rattled against the fence, stealing her from her thoughts. "Entrance," the sign read. She dropped her keys and few other items back in her purse and then pushed the gate open.

The sign should have read "Enter here and risk everything," Casey thought, because as she walked into the stadium that's exactly how she felt.

# 22

## SHIRTLESS

*April 9, 2015*

For some reason the blue-colored track surprised her even though she had seen it before. Casey didn't know if the track was blue because it was the natural color of the material they used or just because this is the University of Florida and everything is either orange or blue. Either way, she kept walking towards the bleachers that were just past the athletic facility.

Casey's shift had ended at six and it took just over thirty minutes to get from Shands Hospital all the way across campus. By the time she sat down on the bleachers, it was already 6:41.

Her plan was fool proof. Except for the fact that she had no clue if they had practice today, or if she was even allowed at practice. She probably should have looked this up online or something, but she didn't. And that's all besides the fact that she had no idea what she was going to say to Ben, if he was even here.

She ran the actual scenario through her head, and it suddenly sounded a lot worse than she realized. *I know I flirted with you, let you kiss me, kissed you back, gave you my number, and then ignored your calls, but I'm actually a really cool girl.*

As Casey sat there the practice seemed unorganized for the most part. Maybe that's because it was nearly finished, but it just looked like a bunch of shirtless guys walking around and stretching. She still hadn't spotted Ben yet, but the track was huge. Actually the track wasn't huge, but the soccer field inside the track was huge. On one end of the soccer field was a strip of track that led to the high jump, and on the other end, a giant circle was cut out of the grass, which Casey guessed was for discus and shot put.

Several guys walked out of the athletic facility and onto the soccer field. It was pretty easy to tell the field guys apart from the track guys. Mainly because they were huge compared to the runners. Several of the runners, however, were actually pretty big as well. Did football players also run track?

She looked down at her phone: 6:52 p.m. She was still the only person in the bleachers, but either the guys walking in and out of the locker rooms didn't see her or they didn't care she was there because no one said anything.

Casey recognized several of the trainers helping some of the guys stretch out. A couple of them were in med school with Nikki, likely building up their resume for residency applications. Most were doing some type of hamstring stretch, lying on their back while the trainer pushed their straightened leg towards them. She had to admit, they were unbelievably flexible.

Several more minutes went by and the field was quickly emptying. Two student managers were stacking orange cones and picking up small orange disks off the ground, but there was only one group of runners still at practice, and Ben wasn't one of them.

One of the female trainers walked off the field with a runner towards the glass doors that led to the training facility. The girl waved at Casey as she passed and Casey waved back. The girl's name was Megan and she was one of Nikki's friends. She looked down at her phone again: 7:03 p.m.

The sun was starting to quickly fall below the bleachers on the east side of the field, directly across from where she sat. Casey stood up and stuffed her phone back into the small pouch on the outside of her purse. *This was a bad idea anyways,* she thought.

She was already halfway down the bleacher steps when a group of runners entered the stadium from the back side, caddy corner to where she was now. They were too far away to see their faces, but she was sure the runner in the front left was Ben. She couldn't describe how she knew, she just knew.

They crossed over the track in a matter of seconds and stopped in the dead center of the infield. The glass doors behind Casey opened again and a young girl came walking out with a green six-bottle carrier in each hand. The orange and white Gatorade logo was etched across all of them.

When she looked back towards the field, most of the guys were walking around with their hands tucked behind their heads. They were likely told their entire running lives that doing this expands their lungs so they can breathe easier. The problem with that line of reasoning is that it really isn't getting the oxygen in that is the problem. Heavy breathing during running is more of a function of getting the carbon dioxide out.

One point for doctors, zero points for runners, Casey thought with a smile.

Her smile quickly faded when she looked to the left of that group to two guys standing upright, one of which was pointing directly at her. It was Ben and Parker.

*Why am I nervous? I came to see him, not the other way around.*

Ben started jogging towards her and she realized again that she had no clue what she was going to say.

He pulled up about ten feet from her and started walking. He was wearing blue nylon shorts with a short runners slit on the side, matching Nike shoes that looked about two sizes too small, and no shirt.

He wasn't drenched, but a sheen of sweat covered his body. The muscles in his legs flexed as he took each step. She knew his body was likely experiencing active hyperemia, an increase in organ blood flow during increased metabolic activity. Casey tried to shut off the doctor part of her brain, but she couldn't.

She could easily make out his vastus medialis, vastus lateralis, and rectus femoris as he moved. Her eyes moved up towards his stomach, and his shorts were pulled just slightly below his waist and she could see the tightness in his illiopsoas. Finally the girl in her took over and what it all boiled down to is he had an unbelievably gorgeous body.

Casey hadn't moved from a row about halfway down the bleacher steps, so when Ben stopped, he was a couple feet below her. He rested his arms on the mid-rail and looked up at her.

Instead of her eyes meeting his, they moved down towards his lips, and a tingling sensation shot up her body.

She could still feel the duality of the warmth and coolness from his lips that night he kissed her.

"I'm sorry, but there's no visitors allowed at practice," Ben said completely expressionless.

Casey suddenly felt incredibly stupid. *I can't believe I let Candy talk me into this.* Without saying anything, she turned and started walking down the stairs. She should have known by the fact that no one else was standing around watching that visitors weren't allowed. But it wasn't even that, it was the way he said it.

Before Casey reached the bottom of the stairs, Ben jogged over and blocked her way. He held his hands up in front of him to stop her. "Hey, that was just a joke."

"It was a bad joke," she said as she stepped around him and towards the gate she had come in.

"Okay, it was a bad joke, but remember I'm not good at jokes. I was just shocked to see you."

Casey turned around and took a couple steps toward him. "I'm sorry. I just…"

"Lost your phone? Got a new number? Probably something along these lines, right?"

Casey smiled. "Let's go with lost my phone." She thought she could see a bit of hurt and disappointment in his eyes behind the light-hearted façade.

"You know this all could have been avoided if a certain girl would stop playing games and just let me take her out."

*I am so not playing games,* she thought. But even as Casey thought it, she realized it wasn't entirely true.

"Benson, this isn't the damn Bachelor," Coach Melvick yelled from mid-field. "Stretch out and then you can go flirt as much as you want."

Ben waved playfully. "Thanks, Coach, that was extremely helpful." He turned back to Casey.

"Okay, so take me out," she said.

Ben looked down at his watch. "It's about seven-fifteen. Give me, like, fifteen minutes and we can go."

Casey bit her lip. "I can't tonight…" Nikki was only supposed to watch Emma until eight.

Ben didn't hesitate, though. "Okay, how about tomorrow morning?"

"You want to take me out tomorrow morning?"

"Does seven a.m. work?"

"Like seven in the morning?"

"Yes, you see, a.m. stands for ante meridiem, which is Latin for before midday. You did go to medical school right?"

Casey rolled her eyes. "I've just never been asked out at seven in the morning before. Where are we going to even go?"

"I'll take that as a yes."

Casey thought about it for a second. She hadn't planned on taking Emma to daycare tomorrow, but a half day would be fine, she thought. "Okay, do you want me to write down my address?"

"Benson Hayes Wilder!" Coach Melvick yelled again.

"Will you text it to me?"

"Okay," Casey said.

"In case you get confused, it's that one number that's been calling the past four days."

"Ha. Ha," Casey said before Ben jogged off.

"Wait," Casey said. "Where are we going?"

Ben didn't turn around.

*Does he not know girls need to know these things?*

# 23

## Ante Meridiem

*April 10, 2015*

Casey had a two-bedroom, one-bathroom house in northwest Gainesville. It was in a small community a little ways away from the hospital. Far enough away to avoid most of the endless foray of house parties, but close enough that she still felt a bit of the college life.

It was 6:53 a.m. when Casey heard a car pull into the driveway. She pulled back the curtains from her window and saw a clay red truck with a yellow trim stripe. Letting the curtain fall back in place, she headed toward the front door.

She walked through the open dining room and sat her cup of coffee down next to the sink. She shook her hands like she was trying to dry them off without a towel. Her body tingled with excitement and the 500 mg of caffeine. Casey was so wired that she thought she could actually feel the caffeine block the adenosine receptors in her brain. *Calm down, calm down, calm down. Holy cow, I should have stopped at my second cup of coffee.*

The knock at the door echoed lightly throughout the house, bringing Casey out of her momentary panic.

As Casey opened the front door she got this sudden feeling like she was forgetting something. That feeling went away when she saw him, though. Ben was wearing jeans with a yellow and brown plaid shirt that was rolled up and tucked in, a brown belt, and brown boots. It was the first time she'd seen him wearing something other than orange and blue workout clothes.

He held out a white Calla Lily and Casey took it, twirling the green stem softly between her fingers.

"You look amazing," Ben said before she could thank him for the flower. She caught his eyes scanning her body. She was wearing light-washed jeggings with a small rip a few inches above her right knee, and a short-sleeve tie-neck off-white blouse.

Casey felt like she couldn't stop smiling, "Thank you."

"But, you can't go barefoot," he said with a smile.

Casey looked down and wiggled her toes. "You didn't know? This is the new look."

"I totally knew. I like to keep up to speed on all the hot fashion trends."

"I had a feeling," Casey smirked. "Let me just put this in water and grab a pair of sandals and I'll be right out."

Ben rubbed the back of his neck. "You might want to make it a pair of shoes that can get a little dirty instead."

Casey thought about it for a moment. *A little dirty? Nikki would die if a guy said that to her.* "Umm, okay. Just give me a minute." She left the door open as she jogged back to the kitchen and grabbed a small vase from under the sink. She placed the flower in it, along with a little bit of water, and then walked back to her bedroom.

Casey looked through her closet quickly. Besides her running shoes, she didn't really have any old shoes. She grabbed a pair of russet ankle boots with a zipper on the side. They weren't old, plus they were Nikki's, but that would have to do for now.

Ben was leaning against the wooden post of the front porch when Casey walked back out. She motioned towards her booties with both hands, "Better?"

"Perfect," Ben said.

As they backed out of the driveway, Casey saw Emma's pink and yellow Playmate trike on the side of the house, and she literally held her breath, hoping Ben didn't notice it. She would tell him about Emma, if this turned into something. For today, though, she just wanted to go on a date with a guy.

# 24

## Peanut and Butter

*April 10, 2015*

They talked a lot as they drove. Well, mainly Ben talked a lot because Casey never stopped asking questions.

During the first thirty minutes she had found out he was originally from Ocala, Florida. He was twenty-four years old and a freshman planning to major in mechanical engineering. He was the number-two ranked runner in the country for the 5000 meter, which turns out to be just over three miles. Some famous runner named Steve Prefontaine was one of the main reasons he started running. His closest friend was Parker Collins, with whom he shared a room at Springs Hall, which she already knew. He liked chocolate, but didn't like ice cream, which she refused to believe. His favorite book was *The Philosopher and the Wolf*, and his favorite movie was *Without Limits,* which also happened to be about Steve Prefontaine.

Above all, though, the freshman thing stuck in her mind more than anything else. She didn't really know any twenty-four year old freshman. "Why didn't you go to college right after high school?" Casey asked. She looked over at Ben as he turned off I-75 and onto State Road 40. It was the first question in the past thirty minutes he hadn't immediately responded to.

"I just had some family stuff come up," Ben said. "And I had this offer to be the mechanic for several of the ranchers out here. I was kind of naturally good at fixing things, and it paid well. So I just kind of hung around for a bit."

It felt like he was hiding something, she thought. But twenty minutes into their first date didn't feel like a good time to start prying. "What made you change your mind about college?"

"Actually Coach Melvick recruited me out of high school. I had originally committed, and when I had to pass, he told me to call him if I ever changed my mind. And that was a little over a year ago now."

"But everything is okay now, with your family?"

"It's…getting there," he said.

She wanted to ask him more about his family, but since she wasn't being entirely upfront about her current family situation she couldn't really blame him for not wanting to talk too much about his.

As they kept talking, Casey noticed things about him. A small portion of his bottom lip was slightly discolored, likely from running in the sun too much. His hair was jet black and a lot longer than that of the other runners. Lastly his eyes were a halcyon marine blue with hint of light green. Almost aquamarine, she thought. And while many people say the eyes are the window to the soul, Casey knew they were also the window to one's genes. Which is why she couldn't help but think how similar they looked to Emma's.

Then Casey noticed something else. On his left wrist he wore what looked like a girl's faded purple hair band.

Casey pointed towards it. "What's that?"

Ben looked out his window as they passed several cows grazing in the pasture. "Those are cows," he said with a smile.

Casey shook her head sarcastically. "Thank you, but I know what cows are."

Ben lifted his left hand off the steering wheel and held it up for a second. "Hey, I was just trying to be helpful."

"I meant, what is that band on your wrist?"

Ben looked down at his wrist and then back up at the road, letting out a deep breath. "Oh, that. That's my magical bracelet." Ben didn't elaborate as if no further explanation was needed. He looked over at Casey, who was staring directly at him.

"Are you really going to make me ask what a magical bracelet is?"

Ben laughed. "Nope."

"Fine, I don't want to know about your fake magical bracelet anyways," Casey said playfully. But the truth is she did want to know.

There was a momentary silence in their conversation and Casey leaned her arm alongside the window. She knew they were somewhere in Ocala, but still had no clue where they were going this early in the morning. Casey watched as they drove past endless lines of brown and white three-board fencing and what she guessed was crops of either peas or beans, or maybe both. She could just barely see Ben's

94

reflection in her window, and he kept looking over at her as she continued to look out the window.

"Why did you ask me out?" she said.

"That feels like a trick question."

"It's not. I just…was curious, I guess."

The bumpy dirt road ended and Ben parked the truck behind a scratched-up two-board fence. He turned and looked directly at Casey. "Why did you come to my practice?"

"I felt bad," Casey said.

"Nope."

"What do you mean, 'Nope'?"

"I mean that's incorrect."

"I'm telling you that's why I went there."

"I'm telling you you're wrong. But if you'd like to know the real reason, I'll be glad to tell you that too."

Casey rolled her eyes. "Sure, enlighten me."

"Because you knew it would be worth it," Ben said. He let his answer sink in for a minute. "And that's the same reason I asked you out."

"Do those lines actually work on girls?" Casey joked.

Ben smiled. "The wrong person says all the wrong things, the right person says all the right things."

"What does that mean?"

"It means it's not about what someone says, it's about the person saying them." Ben turned off the truck and pulled the latch to open his door. "By the way, we're here."

He was already around to her side before she could pull open the door. He closed it behind her and she walked towards the fence. She placed her hands on the top board and looked out at the seemingly endless horizon of land. Two horses looked up from feeding on some hay and started trotting along the fence line towards her.

Ben grabbed something out of the backseat and walked up next to her.

The horses were only several yards from them. "That is Peanut and Butter," Ben said.

Casey laughed at the names. "That can't be their real names."

Ben pointed at them. "That brown one there, with the white blaze between his eyes, is Peanut. And the one next to him, the white Arabian, is butter; she's my favorite."

Ben unzipped the plastic bag in his hands and held out several apple slices.

"We can feed them?"

"*You* most surely can," a voice said from their left. A man that Casey hadn't even noticed was walking along the fence. His right hand was gloved and carrying a hammer, and his left hand was bare and empty. "This other fellow, though, he looks a little rough around the edges. I don't know if I want him around my horses."

Casey looked over at Ben, and he winked at her.

"We don't need no trouble now, old man."

"Old man?" the man said. "Boy I will whoop your ass up and down this green grass." The horses moved away from the fence as the man approached, and went back to grazing near another bale of green and yellow hay.

The man stopped right in front of Ben and they just stood there staring at one another.

"Sir," Casey said, "we're sorry, we were just…"

"No need for you to apologize, miss," the man interrupted. "It's this one here who has some explainin' to do."

A big grin spread across Ben's face and he burst into laughter.

"Boy, I will…" the man started to say, but then he began laughing as well.

Both of them hugged one another and walked back over to the fence.

"Wait, you know each other?" Casey said.

"Well, I should hope so," the man said. "I raised the little bastard. Which means it would be nice if he would stop by more than once a month.

"This is—" Ben started.

The man reached out his hand toward Casey. He was older, maybe in his sixties, dressed in jeans and a long sleeve plaid shirt, both of which hugged his lean frame. "I'm Jim."

Casey shook his hand. It was tan and weathered with a hard callous along his thumb and index finger. "I'm Casey," she said.

Jim turned towards Ben and Casey watched the creases in his skin around his neck and eyes. "*The* Casey?"

Casey looked back to Ben. *You told him about me?*

Ben ignored the question.

"Alright, well, you two enjoy yourselves. I got several hundred more posts to walk, and if you stop by the house, you might just find Diane making one of her famous fruit pies."

"Nice to meet you," Casey said.

"Miss," Jim said touching the brim of his hat as he continued along the fence line, glancing at each post as he passed.

When Jim was out of earshot, Casey looked over at Ben, who was holding out his hand.

"You coming?"

Casey climbed over the fence carefully and hopped down onto the damp ground as Ben's hands wrapped faintly around her waist. She turned around and he pulled his hands away. "So are you going to actually tell me where exactly we are now?"

Ben turned back around towards endless green pasture. "This is where I grew up."

# 25

## TRACK

*April 10, 2015*

Casey followed Ben as they walked across the pasture towards Peanut and Butter. The horses continued to graze until they were about ten feet away.

Ben knelt down and Casey followed suit. Peanut was still grazing, but Butter stopped and looked right at them. "You see how her ears are sticking straight up and slightly angled towards us?"

"Yeah," Casey said.

"And you see how his are more relaxed?"

Casey looked over at Peanut and his ears twitched several times and then rested to the side, almost like the wings of an airplane. "Yeah," she said.

"It's a signal that the horses are relaxed."

"What if they weren't relaxed?" Casey asked.

"Their ears would be pinned flat against their heads."

"And that means they're scared?"

"Scared, or spooked, or just uncomfortable with something around them. You typically don't want to approach a horse like that."

"So, Peanut and Butter have happy horse ears?" Casey said with a smile.

Ben laughed. "Actually, yeah, I think that's a good way to put it. Have you ever been around horses?"

Casey shook her head.

"Okay, when we approach, you're going to hold your hand out like this." Ben put his hand out in front of him palm up. "If he smells or touches your hand with his muzzle, then you can try giving him a piece of apple and petting him. Sound good?

Casey nodded and followed Ben towards Butter.

"Hey, girl," Ben said. Butter sighed, breathing in deeply and letting it out audibly through her nostrils. "I'm happy to see you too, girl."

Ben held his hand out like he had shown Casey, and Butter pressed her muzzle against him. He moved his right hand under her chin as his left hand moved up her cheek and to her neck. He looked back at Casey and tilted his head, motioning her closer.

"I have a friend I want you to meet," he said to Butter. "And she's got some treats for you."

"Hold your hand out," he said to Casey. Ben put two apple slices in her palm and Butter took two steps toward her. Casey could feel the hot air exhale from Butter's nostrils, and then she scooped the two apple slices in with her lips.

Butter sighed again, and Peanut walked over. "You like that, huh?" Casey said.

Ben handed her a couple more apple slices and she fed Peanut too. She stepped forward slightly and ran her hand over his crest and down his neck. "Do they like to be pet?"

"Of course," Ben said. "You just have to find the right spot and put a little muscle behind it. They have thick skin, and getting pet gently sometimes tickles them more than anything."

Casey rubbed her hand firmly down Peanut's neck. It was smooth, but she could also feel subtle striations in his skin. It reminded her of the muscle tissue around the heart, smooth with barely noticeable striations.

Ben fed Butter the last of the apples and held up his hands. "I'm sorry girl, that's all we got." He looked over at Casey. "Now this is the hard part."

"What is?"

"Leaving them."

Casey puffed out her bottom lip into a sad face and gave Peanut one last long stroke down his mane. "Mr. Ben says I have to leave you now. I would stay with you all day, but he says I can't."

They both walked away slowly, farther into the property.

Casey looked back after a couple minutes. "They're still following us."

Ben smiled. "They want more apples." For several more minutes, Casey watched the horses as they walked. Behind them it looked like part of the pasture had been mowed recently because there were long lines of fresh grass shavings. Ahead of them on the right was a cute little red house with white trim. Casey pictured a plump old lady named Diane baking some homemade pie. Possibly even sitting it out on the window sill like they did in movies, the aroma rising like a small smoke stack. They were walking farther away from the house, in the other direction though, towards a large field of corn.

"So, I can't believe you told your dad about me? I must be like super special." Casey joked.

"You mean Uncle Jim?"

"He's your uncle?"

"It's kind of a long story."

"I like long stories," Casey said. She saw a little hesitation in Ben.

"Jim and Diane were my foster parents. Technically they adopted me when I was 13, and I have just always called them Uncle Jim and Aunt Diane. Actually I guess it's not that long of a story."

"Can I ask what happened to your biological parents?"

"You can, but I can't tell you. I mean, I would, but I just don't know."

"What do you mean?"

"I grew up in foster care until I was around twelve, Jim and Diane adopted me about a year later, and other than that no one could ever tell me anything about my parents."

Casey wanted to ask him more about his parents, and about his time growing up here, but she was distracted by tall rows of corn they were fast approaching. "I thought you told Uncle Jim you were taking me to some track?"

A few steps later and the grass ended. They were getting closer to the corn and walking over a dry and dusty soil. Ben stopped nearly ten feet shy of what looked like endless rows of corn. To his left there was an opening about five feet wide. "Welcome to my track," he said.

Casey stopped next to Ben and a small cloud of dust kicked up around her boots.

Ben held out his hand, "Shall we?"

Casey took it and they stepped in between the rows of corn. His hand slid over hers and gently clasped towards the tips of her fingers.

After several steps Ben guided her to the right down another path, and then back to the left. The low angle of the morning sun fell behind the tall stalks of corn as they continued to walk through the dim lit pathways.

Casey looked around as a swift breeze rushed through the corn, tipping the stalks like a pendulum. "What is this place?"

"Jim and Diane moved out here to retire just a couple years before they first took me in. It was mostly just run down farmland then. By the time I came along Jim had started messing around with several different crops, mostly sweet corn and pumpkins."

Ben stopped and knelt down towards the bottom of several corn stalks. He picked up a small orange pumpkin, about the size of a baseball. "The corn will be ready several months before the pumpkins, but they can grow together," he said, holding it up.

Casey looked around. Between each row of corn was a patch of pumpkins. It looked like little orange balls scattered among a forest of corn.

Ben handed Casey the pumpkin and she held it in front of her like she was holding a tiny person in her hand. Emma would love this, she thought.

Casey sat the pumpkin back down. "This is so cool, but what's with all the paths cut into the corn? Is that normal?"

Ben laughed. "No, it's not normal. At least I don't think. I used to love to run through the corn fields each spring. First thing after school I'd come out here. I kind of started damaging some of the pumpkins and corn, and then one day I got a little scraped up. I thought they were going to make me stop, but instead Diane had Jim cut out paths that I could run around."

Ben stood up and brushed off his knees. "It might sound funny, but I love this place."

Casey smiled. She loved that he took her here. She reached out and grabbed his hand as they continued walking. "What do you love so much about running?" she asked.

"I didn't have a lot of constants growing up," he said. "Everything changed every time I moved to a different foster home. It almost felt like starting over each time."

Casey looked up at Ben as they walked and she could see him searching for the right words.

Ben motioned to the path they were walking down. "But for a while, I had this makeshift track. I could run here after school. I could run here in the rain. When the stalks were tall in the spring I could run here, and when they were dead and gone in the fall, I could run here. Whether I had a bad day or a good day, or whether it was hot or cold, it didn't matter. This track was here."

Ben's voice softened. "I know this dirt-filled track better than I know most people. I know it takes me 697 steps at a good mile pace. I know there are twenty-three left turns and only nine right turns if I run it counterclockwise. I know where the corn grows faster each year because the soil is a little better, and where the pumpkins are a little bigger. This corn-field track became my constant. And when I run it's like nothing else exists."

Ben kicked at a small stone in front of him and then he looked down at Casey with a light smile. "Of course, it also helped that I was faster than most everyone too."

"Have you ever lost a race?" Casey asked.

"I didn't really start running competitively until high school, and, yeah, early on I lost a lot. Mainly because I had no clue how to run a race."

"How is it different than running out here?" Casey said.

"The biggest thing for me was learning when to run against the other runners, and when to run against myself."

"What's the difference?"

They took a slight left that led down a diagonal path that was narrower than the previous ones.

"You really want to know this? I feel like I'm boring you with all this running stuff."

"No, I like it," Casey said. "I mean, I love to run too, but the way you talk about it makes it seem so different."

"Okay, well, when I first started running, I would kind of just run as fast as I could for as long as I could. This is what my coach referred to as running against yourself."

"And that's bad?" Casey said.

"Well, most of the time, yes. When you just run all out, it's called front running. It's not that front running is bad necessarily. It just takes a lot more effort. Mainly because you're the one cutting through the wind, which allows the other runners to draft off you. They can essentially just hang back, conserve energy, and out sprint you at the end. They call that dropping the hammer or the kick."

"So you were a front runner?"

"I was."

"But you changed?" Casey said, completely intrigued.

"I did."

Casey grinned "And now you drop the hammer?"

"I do."

"So basically, I'm now a running expert?"

"I would have to say so," Ben said laughing.

They walked down the path for several more minutes, taking two more left turns several hundred feet apart. The sun had risen enough to cast a shadow of corn stalks that danced with theirs as they walked.

Ben turned right and slowed down. There was a large square opening in front of them, a little bit bigger than a bedroom. Every side except for where they were standing was a giant wall of corn, and in the middle was a blue and white cooler, the familiar words *Coleman* engraved on the side.

Ben walked over to the cooler and picked up the cream vanilla blanket that was folded neatly on top. He unfolded it and fanned it over the grassy opening, sat down and opened up the cooler.

Casey was still standing there watching when he pulled out two small mason jars, two spoons, and two bottles of water. She sat down, crossed her legs out in front of her and leaned over on her right elbow. She was thinking back on her life. "I don't think I've ever actually been on a real picnic," she said.

Ben smiled. "Are you hungry? I've got homemade parfaits, with yogurt, granola, blueberries, and strawberries."

Casey was hungry. Actually she was starving. She looked down at the jars with their little silver metal lids. There just one problem, she was allergic to strawberries.

106

"What's wrong?" Ben asked.

"Promise not to hate me?"

Ben laughed. "That is ominous, but I promise."

"I'm allergic to strawberries," she said.

Ben sat up on his knees and put both glasses back in the cooler. He turned towards Casey. "I'm pretty sure it was someone in the Navy Seals that coined the term 'two is one, and one is none.' I always liked that motto. But I figured if having a Plan B is good, then having a Plan C, D, must be twice as good, right?"

Casey nodded, though wasn't quite following.

Ben pulled out a plate of something concealed by aluminum foil. He uncovered the plate slightly, "For Plan B we have pumpkin chocolate chip muffins, courtesy of Aunt Diane."

Casey thought it was cute and endearing every time he called her 'Aunt Diane.'

Ben reached back in the cooler and pulled out another plate covered in tin foil. "For Plan C we have fruit kabobs." He looked down at them, "Though you may have to pull the strawberries off."

"And last, but not least, and also my personal favorite: monkey balls!"

Casey laughed. "Please tell me you did not just say monkey balls."

Ben looked at her wide-eyed. "Oh my gosh. Have you never had a monkey ball?"

"That might officially be the weirdest thing anyone has ever said to me."

Ben looked around at the corn and cupped his hands around his mouth. "Ladies and gentlemen. We have before us a monkey ball newcomer."

"Are they really called monkey balls?"

"Uh yes, and they are amazingly delicious."

Casey reached out to lift the tin foil on the plate covering the monkey balls, but Ben pulled them out of her reach.

"Woah there, tenderfoot," Ben said.

"The monkey ball experience is not something to be rushed. This is a day that you will cherish for the rest of your life."

Casey bit her bottom lip trying not to laugh, because Ben's expression was completely serious.

"First, do you have any other food allergies that I need to know of?"

"Avocado for sure, and I was warned to avoid papaya and chestnut, but I've never had those."

Ben breathed out an audible sigh and looked up towards the clouds. "The monkey ball gods shine down on us this day."

"C'mon, nothing named monkey balls can be that good?"

"Close your eyes," Ben said.

Casey sat up on her knees and closed her eyes. "You promise this isn't some weird food thing, right?" She heard the metallic crinkle of the tin foil, and felt the blanket below her shift as Ben moved closer.

"No peaking," Ben said as she opened her right eye for just a second. "Okay, on the count of three I'm going to place the monkey ball against your lips to take a bite."

Casey nodded.

"Okay, one…two…three."

Ben pressed it against her lips and Casey bit into the little ball of dough that was baked with ground cinnamon, melted butter, and sugar. She opened her eyes and looked at Ben while she finished chewing.

"Well?" he said.

"Oh. My. Gosh. It was like eating a little bit of heaven."

Ben laughed as he sat the plate down in front of her. "I told you!"

Casey picked up another. It kind of looked like a cinnamon sugar donut hole, but tasted richer. "How have I not heard of these?"

"There's actually one more thing," Ben said.

Casey finished chewing her second one, little pieces of cinnamon and sugar sticking to her lips. "What's that?"

"Now, I didn't make this up. I'm just reciting to you the monkey ball rules. It clearly states that a first time monkey ballee, must award the monkey baller with a kiss on the cheek."

Casey smiled and squinted her eyes playfully. "Is that so?"

"I'm just telling you exactly like I was told so many years ago."

Casey wiped the crumbs from her fingers and leaned over towards Ben so that she was on all fours, just a few inches from his lips. She arched her back just barely as she looked at him. "You wouldn't lie to an innocent girl just to get a kiss would you?"

"Never," Ben said, almost in a whisper.

Casey moved closer to his lips and at the last second turned to the left slightly and pressed her lips against his right cheek.

"Now if there are no other rules, please pass me another monkey ball."

Both Casey and Ben laughed as they sat there enjoying the rest of a slow Saturday morning.

# 26

## He Knows

*April 10, 2015*

Casey was unusually quiet most of the drive home. The image of Ben running through the half grown corn fields as a kid was repeating over and over in her head. He seemed so passionate about running; it had been such an impactful part of his life. And yet she couldn't help but think his story seemed lonely.

Ben reached across the seat, and the touch of his hand startled her. He went to pull it back, but she took his hand and held it close to her. She ran her fingers over the back of his hand, and traced softly up and down each of the metacarpal bones. It made her think of an anatomy mnemonic for the carpal bones that seemed to fit her and Ben's story perfectly: She Looks Too Pretty, Try To Catch Her. *Did he catch me?*

Ben let go of her hand as he pulled into the driveway. He put the truck in park and turned towards her. "Is something wrong?" he asked.

*Yes, I have a daughter and I'm afraid to tell you because you won't like me, which actually makes no sense because if you don't like me because of my daughter then I don't want to be anywhere near you to begin with. Aghh!*

Casey didn't know what to say, so she just said it. "I have a daughter." She didn't even look at him as she said it. Instead she sat there like she'd just thrown a grenade and was taking cover, minus the whole part about sticking your fingers in your ears and curling up into a little ball. Though both of those things were sounding like decent options.

"I know," Ben said.

Casey immediately turned towards him in shock. Like maybe he didn't hear her, or maybe the grenade just hadn't gone off yet. So, she threw it again.

"I think you might have misheard me. I have a daughter." This time she drew out the word "daughter" like she was talking to a child.

Ben laughed. "I knoooowwww," he said, mocking her.

"I don't get it. How can you know? And why didn't you tell me you knew? And why did you go out with me if you knew? How can you possibly know?"

Ben was laughing as he listened to Casey. He unbuckled his seat belt and shifted his weight so he was leaning over his right leg, closer to her. "Come here," he said.

Casey scooted over a bit and sat there, still waiting for the answers to her questions.

"First I'm going to kiss you, because you look unbelievably cute all worked up."

His lips were already pressing into hers before she could protest to being "all worked up." His right hand lightly

112

touched the bottom of her chin as he held the kiss for several seconds.

"I'm not worked up," she lied the moment his lips left hers. "But I really do have a daughter."

Ben held her gaze as he spoke. "When I got here this morning, I noticed the tricycle at the side of the house." Ben tilted his head in the direction where the bike was still lying in the grass.

"That could have been the neighbors, though, or…"

"Or maybe you just like to cruise around town on your cute little pink tricycle?"

Casey squinted her eyes at him. "Ha. Ha. So, you figured from the bike I had a daughter."

"Well, it is pink with nice bright pink streamers, so I kind of ruled out son."

"Maybe I was just babysitting for someone and they left it here by accident?"

"Honestly that just doesn't seem probable. But, that wasn't what gave it away."

Casey tried to think about what he might have seen in the house, but nothing came to mind. Most of the pictures of her and Emma were in the hallway to her room, and there were a few things in the kitchen. She had also cleaned up the living room and her room and knew there weren't any toys or anything lying around. But none of that mattered anyways because he never even went inside. "Then what was it?"

"The egg."

"The egg?" Casey said, trying to figure out what he was talking about. *Crap, the Easter egg. The one Emma painted a few weeks ago at school was still sitting on the table…by the front door.*

113

"So, a painted egg and a tricycle and you figured I had a daughter?"

"That and you're different."

"I'm different? How am I different?

"If I tell you that now, then what will we have to talk about at dinner on Monday?"

"And what makes you think I'll go out with you again?" Casey said, fighting back a smile.

Ben didn't take his eyes off of her as he asked, "Will you go to dinner with me Monday night? I promise no strawberries."

Casey thought about it for a second, even though she already knew her answer. She opened the passenger side door. "Will you walk me to the door?"

Casey walked around the front of the truck and Ben walked her to the front porch. She slid her key into the lock and turned around. "I'm supposed to work until six on Monday. How about I give you a call after and we can grab something to eat?"

Ben smiled. "Sounds perfect."

Casey turned the lock clockwise and pulled down on the handle.

As she opened the door and stepped inside, Ben said, "Casey."

She looked back at him.

"I had a lot of fun today."

"Me too," Casey said.

When she was inside she leaned her back against the door and sighed already looking forward to Monday.

# 27

## Cool Ranch

*April 10, 2015*

Casey's back was still against the door when she heard the old truck engine start up and back out of the driveway.

"These chips are stale," Nikki said walking out of the kitchen. She crunched down on another cool ranch Dorito and Casey nearly screamed.

"What?" Nikki said, her mouth half full of Doritos. She pointed to the bag. "You weren't saving these were you?"

"You nearly gave me a heart attack. "What are you doing here?"

"I'm sorry, but my roommates were driving me absoposilutely crazy." She walked over to the couch and Casey followed. "Seriously," she went on. "They never stop studying."

"It's med school," Casey said. "That's kind of the point."

Nikki stopped eating and looked Casey up and down. "Umm, why are you all dressed up?"

Casey smiled and bit down on her lip.

Nikki dropped the bag of chips and ran to the window. She spread the blinds apart and looked out. "Was he here?"

"Mayyybeee," Casey said.

"How could you not tell me?" Nikki yelled.

"I was nervous. I just didn't want it to be a big deal."

"And?"

"And it was amazing."

Casey told Nikki about Aunt Diane and Uncle Jim, and Peanut and Butter, and the corn field, and the breakfast. When she got to the part about the monkey balls Nikki didn't even question it. She just sat there eating one chip after another like it was popcorn and she was watching a movie. By the time Casey was done it felt like she had been talking for hours.

"So let me get this straight. Not only did you just go on a date with a super hot college athlete. But he's an engineer and a cowboy?" Nikki looked around the room like she was lost. Then she reached over and pinched Casey on the arm.

"Ow!" Casey yelled. "What was that for?"

"Sorry, I just wanted to make sure this was real life."

# 28

## SILENT

*April 13, 2015*

Parker jogged alongside Ben as they began their twenty-fourth and final lap for the day. Coach had called for an "easy ten," which meant 10,000 meters and they weren't allowed to run it faster than forty minutes. That was just over seven minutes per mile, so it was just a nice jog for most of the guys.

"Seriously, how did it go on Saturday?" Parker asked again.

Ben gave the same answer he had for the last twenty times Parker asked. "It went fine."

"Fine? Seriously? You were obsessed with taking this girl out, and all I get is an 'it went fine?' How fine? Fine as in you probably won't see her again? Fine as in she's a bit of a freak and you guys had wild barn sex?"

Ben looked over at Parker, "What the heck is wild barn sex?"

"I don't know, man, I'm trying to live vicariously through you right now and you won't let me!"

"Vicariously?"

"Yes, man, I've been brushing up on my vocab. Girls like the smart guys these days."

"Last week you told me girls liked guys majoring in agriculture, and the week before you were convinced it was all about wearing your visor backwards and upside down like you were Karch Kiraly."

"Girls are fickle, man, you gotta go with the flow," Parker said.

"You realize you have mental problems, right?"

Parker and Ben jogged across the finish line and pulled up in the grass infield as the rest of the team followed suit. Even though it was an easy pace, everyone was sucking wind. Between breaths, Ben said, "If you must know…I asked her out again for tonight…but …she hasn't called me yet…so…I don't even know what the deal is."

Parker grinned, "Man, this is good."

"How is this good?"

"Well, not for you. But, I mean, for me. I figure if you're having problems with girls, then at least I'm not the only one."

Ben just shook his head.

They stretched out and then hit the showers. With the last meet of the season coming up, Coach cut the practice short.

With a towel wrapped around his waist, Ben opened the door to his locker and pulled out his phone. It was 6:09, and she still hadn't called. In fact she hadn't texted or called since their date on Saturday. Of course, he hadn't either though. What was the protocol these days?

"Yo, Ben!" Parker yelled, throwing a towel at him. Instead of hitting Ben, the towel knocked his phone out of his hand.

"What the hell, man?"

"Dude, calm down. Coach has been yelling your name while you're lost in your own little world over there."

Ben pulled on a pair of shorts and shirt, slipped on some flip-flops, and walked out of the locker room towards Coach's office.

# 29

## Overcome

*April 13, 2015*

When Ben reached the door to Coach's office, he walked right in; Coach Melvick couldn't stand formality. He was probably the only athletic head at UF that didn't decorate his office with trophies and awards of all the previous years. It definitely wasn't for a lack of achievements either, UF having been the Division 1 Men's Track and Field Runner-up in 2004, 2005, 2014, and the Champion 2012 and 2013. Nope, all Coach had were a stack of yellow legal pads with tons of hand-scribbled notes about his runners and an orange and blue betta fish that his wife gave him.

"Shut the door behind you, Ben," Coach said.

Ben took a seat in one of the blue leather chairs across from his desk. To Ben's right was a brunette lady sitting against the adjacent wall, wearing a black pantsuit with a white blouse, and clutching a leather bound notebook.

"You wanted to see me, Coach?" Ben said, ignoring the woman in the room for the moment.

Coach didn't say anything at first, he just leaned back in his chair and folded his hands in his lap. He looked annoyed about something.

"Ben, this is Claire Stewart," Coach said. He didn't motion at the woman, or even look at her. He just stared straight ahead at Ben.

Ben looked over at Ms. Stewart. She looked middle aged, maybe late thirties. Her hair was pulled up in a ponytail with long bangs cropping her face, and a pair of glasses tucked into her blouse. Ben was unsure if he should cordially introduce himself or half pretend she wasn't even in the room like Coach. The woman flashed a quick closed lip smile, and he chose to do the same.

"Miss Stewart here is a journalist for the local ABC affiliate." Coach paused again, seemingly forcing his sentences out through gritted teeth. "She plans to run a story in the near future."

Ben tried to remain expressionless as his hands clamped tightly around his legs, as if he were bracing for impact. It hadn't been abnormal for reporters to request interviews, but Coach was making this particular one seem like a big deal.

"She is here out of the kindness of her cold, black heart to let us know in advance," Coach seethed.

It would be an understatement to say Coach definitely did not like this woman, or the reason she was here.

The woman who had been sitting silently in the corner of the room began to speak: "Ben." Her voice didn't seem hurtful or mean. In fact it was soft and slow and poured out like a stream of cool water. "I want to tell your story."

Ben looked over at the woman's dark brown eyes but didn't respond.

She continued. "I want to tell the story of the young man who returns to running to shatter several collegiate records, after overcoming the tragic loss of his daughter and wife…"

The woman kept on talking about something, possibly even asking Ben questions. Ben still stared in the woman's direction, but he didn't see her. He didn't hear her. All he heard was Grace's voice. All he saw was her aquamarine eyes.

# 30

## STORY

*June 9, 2014*

"Will you tell me a story?"

"Sure," Ben said. Have you ever heard about the tortoise and the hare?"

Grace shook her head no. "I want to hear a story about you running."

"Well, this is even better. It's a story about why I used to run."

A look of excitement spread across Grace's face. She grabbed Baby Bear and pulled him close to her chest.

"Long ago, in a land not so far away, there was the race of all races when a tortoise challenged a hare."

"What's a hare?" Grace asked.

"It's a larger version of a rabbit. Very, very fast."

"What's a tortoise?"

"It's a larger version of a turtle."

"Is it fast?"

"Well, that's a question that you'll have to answer after you hear the story."

"Okay, keep going."

"A couple weeks prior to the race not a single person believed the tortoise could win because the hare was known as the fastest animal in all the land. The tortoise wasn't very happy that no one believed in him, but he didn't let it bother him.

"On the day of the race the hare offered to give the tortoise a head start, but the tortoise declined. So, when the race started the hare took off so fast that he left the tortoise spinning in his shell.

"The race was long though. It was through miles and miles of forest, and about half way through the hare was getting hungry. So, he stopped under a shade tree and ate a few carrots. He thought that since he was so much faster than the tortoise, he could rest and still have plenty of time to win."

Grace turned over on her side and pulled the blanket up over Baby Bear.

"But…making his way through the race was the tortoise. He was determined to never stop, to give everything he had until the very end. And after a little while he passed the hare asleep under the shade tree.

"He was hungry too, and carrots sounded delicious, but he didn't stop. He kept on going.

"About an hour later the hare woke up, thinking he'd only been asleep for a few minutes. But the other animals told him the tortoise had passed by here a long time ago. The hare jumped up frantically and took off, running even faster than before.

"He finally caught the tortoise just a few steps short of the finish line. Thinking he could easily pass the tortoise he slowed down just enough to wave to the crowd. But that was a big mistake because the tortoise stretched out his neck at the last second and crossed the finish line one inch ahead of the hare."

"The tortoise won?" Grace said.

"He did."

"But how, if the hare was so much faster?"

"Because the tortoise never gave up, and that is the most important thing of all."

Grace thought about it for a moment and then asked, "Did you ever give up?"

# 31

## The Past

*April 13, 2015*

Ben sat there staring at Claire Stewart's empty seat, even as she walked out of Coach's office. He still hadn't said a word since he'd walked into the room.

Coach leaned forward in his chair and rested his elbows over the hard wooden desk. He muttered, "This is complete bullshit. People going around, digging in another person's past like it's just scraps of garbage to be tossed about. I'm calling the AD and we're going to put a stop to this shit." Coach swiveled in his chair and picked up the phone.

"No," Ben said.

Coach slowly put the phone down and looked across his desk at his star athlete.

"This is *your* life, kid. Not theirs."

Ben lowered his head and let out a deep breath. Then he looked up at Coach. "The past cannot be changed by words. It cannot be made better by sensationalism or worse by

126

simplification. We are all challenged daily to accept our past, and mine shouldn't be any different."

Ben stood up and walked towards the door.

"How do you want to handle the team?" Coach asked.

Ben hesitated. Coach and Parker were the only ones who knew about his past. "I want to tell them."

Ben closed the door behind him, and Coach looked over at the fish just sitting there in his little bowl. "Tough little son of a bitch, isn't he?"

* * *

Parker was still sitting there, thumbing through his phone when Ben walked back to his locker.

"What did Coach want?"

Ben grabbed his dirty clothes and tossed them in the laundry bin a few feet away. "There was a reporter," Ben said as he re-folded a shirt that was sitting in the bottom of his locker.

"What did he want?"

"She," Ben corrected.

"Okay, what did *she* want?"

"She's going to run a story about me."

"Like about your recent records and what not?"

Ben grabbed his phone off the top shelf of his locker and looked over at Parker. "Yeah." He paused, looking down at his hands and then back up at Parker. "And about Amanda and Grace."

Parker straightened up and slid his phone in his pocket. "You okay with that? Because I don't give a flying fuck who it is, I'll go put a stop to it right now.

For all of Parker's faults and shortcomings Ben could never say he wasn't loyal.

"I appreciate it, but it's okay. I'm gonna tell the guys before practice tomorrow, and then she can run her story."

"You sure?" Parker asked.

Ben looked back down at his hands, but this time they were clinched. Without warning his right arm went back and his fist exploded towards the locker next to his. The painted blue metal caved in, folding up one of the hinges.

Jimmy walked around the corner. "What the hell man? That's my locker."

Ben turned around and started walking towards Jimmy, his right fist clinched and now bleeding. Parker cut him off though and started pushing him towards the door. He looked back at Jimmy. "Jimmy get the fuck out of here." Jimmy didn't move. "Now!"

Jimmy walked out of the locker room opposite of where Parker was standing in front of Ben. But before Parker could do anything else Ben stormed out of the locker room.

\* \* \*

Ten minutes later and Ben was about halfway back to his dorm. He didn't really want to go back to his dorm. His mind was focused on two things. One of them he didn't have the energy to confront, and the other was Casey Taylor.

As if on cue Ben's phone started to buzz in his pocket. "Hello?" he said.

"Hey, it's Casey."

The second she spoke, Ben knew something was wrong.

"I was beginning to wonder if you were going to call," he said.

"Sorry, I got held up at work for a few minutes."

"No problem, you still in the mood to grab a bite to eat?"

"Actually, I'm starving, but…"

There it was. The "but." Quite possibly the worst word in the entire English language. To date, not a single person has managed to put together a positive comment after saying the word "but." Tonight wasn't any different.

"…I can't tonight," Casey finished.

"Is everything alright?" Ben asked.

"Everything is fine, and I've been looking forward to tonight, but…"

*Seriously? I hate that word.*

"I'm sorry I couldn't find a sitter."

*Wait…that's not a big deal.*

"Do you like pizza?" Ben said.

"Umm, yes. Why?"

"Does your daughter like pizza?" Ben said.

"Yes…why?"

Ben knew what he was about to say was risky. He also knew something she didn't: He was great with kids.

"Do you have any beach chairs?"

"Ummm, I have a few, but why?"

"Okay. I've got an idea, if you trust me."

There was a hesitation on her end. Then she said, "Okay."

Ben could tell she was nervous. He didn't know how many guys she'd dated since her daughter was born. He didn't know how many of them had met her or if it went good or bad. However, he did know she was taking a chance on him, and right now it was something he needed more than anything.

# 32

## Familiar

A half hour later Ben pulled into Casey's driveway, put the truck in park, and looked into the rear-view mirror. He caught sight of the look in his eyes and realized this wasn't the same type of nervous he got before each race. The excited nervous he had on their first date was gone. This was more of a scared nervous.

His thoughts drifted back to Grace for a moment as he sat there silently in the truck. He wondered if Casey's daughter would be anything like Grace, and what it would feel like to be with Casey around her.

The slight movement of the front door opening pulled him back to the present. Casey stepped through the threshold and leaned against the door jamb. She was wearing a dark navy dress that stopped several inches above her knee, and had a small column of four gold buttons that ran vertically up from her waist. The bottom of the dress fell soft and lose against her legs, but the top seemed to hug every curve and

131

facet of her body. It accentuated her tight waist, and every thought he had for a moment was about wrapping his arms around her.

The scoop neck top was flatteringly modest, while the thin straps on her shoulders revealed her unbelievably sexy arms. *That is definitely an underappreciated part of the female body.*

Her blonde hair was down and fell just below her shoulders. She looked absolutely stunning except for one thing: she wasn't smiling.

It probably had to do with the fact that he was still sitting in the truck, looking more hesitant than excited. Maybe she was thinking this was a mistake.

Ben reached over to the passenger side and picked up the pizza from Papa John's, and two red roses from Flowers By Edie.

Casey smiled the second he stepped out of the car, and for what felt like the first time since he pulled into her driveway, he breathed. He carried the pizza box like a waiter in his left hand, while his right held onto the flowers. Just before he reached Casey he rested one of the flowers on the box so he could hand the other one to her.

She took it with both hands. "Thank you, it's beautiful."

"Hopefully the other lady of the house will think so as well," he said.

Her smile faded at the sound of his words. "Ben," she said looking up at him. She was going to warn him that meeting Emma isn't like meeting a friend or a parent. It is so much more. And once he does this, there is no going back. Everything will change.

"I know," he said, as if reading her mind.

Her lips parted for a second as she breathed in deeply. He knew it wasn't the right time, but the way her lips moved, the sound of her breath. All he wanted right now was to kiss her.

The door moved behind Casey and two little bare feet appeared. "Mom, what are you doing out here?"

Casey stepped to the side and Ben saw Emma for the first time. Her resemblance to Casey was uncanny. Her nose, her ears, her mouth, the shape of her face. It all matched her mother's perfectly. All, except for one thing: her eyes. They were similar to Casey's deep blue, but with a familiar hint of green. Almost aquamarine, Ben thought.

Casey held out her hand. "Emma, come here, I want you to meet someone."

Emma walked over to her mom and took her hand, her head coming up just above Casey's waist.

"This is Mr. Ben, the man I was telling you about."

Ben knelt down and held out the other rose. "I didn't know what your favorite flower was, but I got you this rose."

Emma took the flower and held it up in front of her with both hands just as Casey had done. "It is very pretty, but I like blue ones the best."

Ben smiled as he knelt there looking back at Emma. He couldn't help but feel there was something so incredibly familiar about her. "I'll remember that for next time," he said.

He stood back up. "Is everyone hungry for some pizza?"

Casey looked down at Emma, who was shaking her head up and down with a big grin. "I'll take that as a yes," Casey said.

He looked down at Emma again. The whole thing with the reporter must have gotten to him more than he thought. Because this time he realized why the greens and blues that danced in her eyes looked so familiar. They reminded him of Grace.

Emma nodded and Ben started walking back towards his truck.

"Wait. Where are you going?"

"It's a surprise. But I need the chairs." Casey looked completely confused when he turned back around. "Are they in the garage?"

"Is what in the garage?"

"Stay with me now, the beach chairs. You *are* the girl I talked to on the phone a half-hour ago right?"

"Yes…I just…the chairs are in the garage. I'll open it and fix some drinks."

"Okay, but one more thing." Ben walked back up to her and kissed her quickly and without hesitation. "I've been wanting to do that since I saw you tonight." Ben drew an X over his heart with his index finger as he backed down the walkway. "I won't do that with Emma around, cross my heart."

# 33

## COUNTING CARS

*April 13, 2015*

A few minutes later and Casey walked through the garage carrying three glasses of water, with Emma next to her carrying a roll of paper towels and some paper plates. All she could do was laugh when she found Ben sitting in a chair in the bed of his truck.

He stepped down and grabbed the glasses from her, then hopped back up on the tailgate and sat one in each of the cup holders attached to the folding chairs. Then he turned around and held out his hand.

Casey gave him the standard you-want-us-to-have-a-picnic-in-my-driveway-in-the-back-of-your-truck look.

Ben responded with the standard guy look, which pretty much never changes.

She reached up and grabbed Ben's hand and stepped up on the tailgate next to him. Casey turned around to grab Emma, but was surprised to see Ben already motioning to help her up. She was worried how Emma might react.

"Your turn," Ben said to Emma. "Now reach your hands straight to the sky. You ready?"

Emma nodded holding her arms up like she was Superwoman.

Ben grabbed her by the wrists and lifted her straight up on to the tailgate. He held his hand up in the air, "Good job. Hi-five."

She slapped his hand and he moved it down by his feet. "Down low?"

She went to slap it again, but he moved it just in time. "You're too slow."

"Hey," she said. "You moved it."

Ben laughed, and Casey smiled. *Guys are so weird.*

"Are you a pepperoni or cheese type of girl?" Ben asked, still kneeling in front of Emma.

"Pepperoni, please."

"I knew it. You have that special pepperoni-girl look. Grab a seat by your mom and I'll get you a slice."

Emma sat down in the chair on the far end, next to Casey, who was sitting in the middle still watching the exchange. "Can I have two slices?" she said as Ben opened up the box.

"You can, but…only if you tell me a secret."

Ben put two slices of pepperoni on a plate and turned to face Emma.

"What kind of secret?" she asked.

"That's up to you."

Emma tapped her index finger against her chin and looked up to the sky, as if she were mimicking someone she'd seen on television deep in thought. Then she blurted out. "I kissed a boy at school today."

Casey literally almost fell out of her chair as Ben handed her the pizza. "You did?" Ben said, giving Casey a little squeeze on the leg to try and calm her. He knew exactly what she was thinking.

Emma pulled off a piece of pepperoni and ate it. "Mhmm."

Casey's mouth was still wide open in absolute shock. Ben lifted his hand off her leg and tapped the bottom of her chin playfully. She looked down at him like he was a great magician that had just performed the best trick of the century. *How did he get her to say that?*

"Does this boy have a name?" Ben said.

Emma shook her head yes as she took a bite of pizza.

Ben handed Casey a plate with one slice of pepperoni and one slice of cheese. Then he put three slices of cheese on his plate and sat down next to her. "Let me guess," he said. "Was his name Rover?"

Emma shook her head again.

"Hmmm, what about Spot?"

"Those are dog names," she said laughing.

"Okay, what about Biscuit?"

"That's not a boy's name either."

"Well, I don't know then. I'm all out of ideas."

"It was Joe."

"Joe Clemmons?" Casey said quickly. Her tone changed, "Emma, you know you're too young to be kissing boys, right?"

"It was just a game."

Ben put the half-eaten pizza down on his plate. "Speaking of games. I have a game we can all play. My uncle and I used to sit out by the road in lawn chairs around the time people got off work and watch the cars go by. I always liked to try and guess the color of the next car, so he made it into a little game. We'd each pick a color and the first person to five wins."

"Sounds fun, doesn't it, Emma?" Casey said.

Emma nodded, but appeared to be more concerned with licking the cheese and sauce off her fingers than anything else.

"Okay, I'll pick red," Casey said.

"I want blue," Emma said.

"Perfect, I will take purple," Ben added.

Casey smiled. Red and blue make purple, she thought.

It was just a few seconds before the first car turned down their street and drove by. "First car," Ben said excited. "And…it's …white. Boo."

Two more cars drove past. One was a light blue Honda that looked like it might breakdown at any moment and the other was a blue Ranger. "Two points for Emma," Ben said.

There was a minute of silence between all three of them as they watched patiently for the next car to drive by. Then Emma spoke. "This is weird."

Ben leaned forward in his chair so he could look over at Emma. "But it's fun, right?"

Emma giggled, "Yeah."

Casey couldn't have said it better herself. The fact that they were sitting in her driveway, in the back of a pickup truck, in beach chairs, eating pizza was a little weird. But, it was also fun and strangely peaceful. A lot of the time dinner inside is filled with so much noise that can't escape the walls around you. Out here though, the world seemed to absorb everything, until there was a stillness internally.

Casey looked over at Ben, who was mid-bite of his second piece of pizza. He stopped with the pizza half in his mouth, "Wha—?"

Casey laughed. "Are you throwing this game?"

He finished his bite. "What do you mean?"

"Purple?"

"What's wrong with purple? I love purple."

"Another car is coming," Emma said.

They both turned and looked. It was red.

"Woohoo. One point for me. That's two for Emma, one for me, and a big fat zero for Ben," Casey said.

"Hey, it's not over yet," Ben defended.

"Name even one thing that's purple."

"Emma's chair is purple," he said with a big grin.

"That doesn't count."

"Okay, fine. Eggplants are purple, cabbage can be purple, butterflies are purple, Barney is purple, sapphires are purple. There's purple people eaters, according to Sheb Wooley, soldiers can receive a purple heart, relish is purple, Lavender is purple, and…being a doctor and all you'll especially like this one…mitochondria is purple."

"That's an odd amount of knowledge about purple, but that doesn't change the fact that a single purple car isn't going to drive by tonight."

"It sounds like somebody wants to make a friendly bet."

"It's not betting if you know you're going to win," Casey said.

"Okay, okay. Then how about this." Ben pulled his phone out of his pocket. It was 7:37 p.m. He had about twenty minutes until sunset and then maybe fifteen minutes more until it was dark. "If a purple car doesn't drive down this street by eight, then you win."

"And what do I win?"

Ben winked. "That's up to you."

Casey thought about it for a moment. "Fine. If a purple car doesn't drive past us by eight *tonight*," she said, thinking he might be trying to pull a fast one. "Then you have to clean my garage."

Ben laughed. "Girls are so bad at this."

"Huh? How is that bad?"

Ben leaned in and whispered in her ear. "If a purple car *does* drive down this street by eight *tonight,* then…"

Casey's eyes opened wide when he finished the sentence. "No way."

Two more cars passed. One black, one blue, but none of them said anything.

"So, do we have a bet?"

"No way. I can't do that," Casey said in a hushed tone.

"Not so confident anymore huh?"

Casey thought about the bet for a moment. It's not that she didn't *want* to do what he was suggesting if he won…it's just, well, it wasn't something she thought she could do. Nikki on the other hand would do something like this even without a bet. She looked at Ben, still grinning in confidence, but there is no way a purple car was driving by. "Fine," she said.

Ben held out his hand to shake on it.

"But…not only do you have to clean my garage, but you also have to mow the front lawn, and…give me a foot massage."

Ben bent over and looked down at her feet tucked inside a pair of brown sandals. "So let me get this straight. If I lose, I have to clean your already clean garage, mow your tiny lawn and then massage your cute feet?

"Yes?"

They shook on it. "Deal," Ben said.

"Deal," Casey said. She looked over at Emma who had been strangely quiet for the past few minutes. She was curled up in the chair sound asleep. Casey tapped Ben on the shoulder and he looked over at her and smiled.

They talked quietly for several minutes, watching the stars fill the dusty sky one by one. A light April breeze stirred several fallen leaves from the small Maple tree in her front yard. To the right, just past Archer Road was a line of tall pines and in between them they could see the myriad of oranges and yellows from the setting sun.

"I'm sorry you had to lose the bet," Ben said.

Casey looked around. "Did I miss the invisible purple car that drove by?"

"No, you just didn't see the one sitting at the park across the street when we made the bet."

Casey immediately looked down the street and to the right a bit where there was a small community park, which was more or less a swing set, a jungle gym, and a basketball hoop. She didn't see a car, though, let alone a purple car. She looked back at Ben, "Good one."

"Look, here it comes now."

Casey looked back again, but still didn't see a purple...wait...on the sidewalk was one of Casey's neighbors. She was wearing the same cut-off jean shorts, aqua green tank top, and cowboy hat that she wore every single day. And of course she had a glass of wine in her hand. As annoying as she was, though, that wasn't the problem. Riding in front of her was her three-year-old daughter wearing nothing but her diaper. Again, not a problem. The problem was she was riding in a purple Power Wheels toy car. Casey didn't take her eyes off the car. "That so does not count."

"It so does."

* * *

Casey walked back outside after she got Emma to brush her teeth and get ready for bed.

Ben had stacked the chairs back up in the garage and was closing the tailgate to his truck. He walked around to the front of his truck and leaned against it, looking at Casey as she walked towards him.

She walked right up to him, ran her hands over his stomach lightly tugging on his shirt, leaned up and kissed him. "She loved you," Casey said, every part of her body smiling. "Only problem is now she wants to know when you're coming over to play again."

Before he could respond, Casey went on. "Seriously, though. I can't believe she kissed a boy! And I can't believe she told you! Where did you come up with that *tell me a secret* thing?"

Ben hesitated. He thought back to Claire Stewart's words from a few hours ago. *I want to tell your story.* He wanted to tell Casey…but he couldn't.

He looked straight into her eyes and his tone was dead serious. "Is there something you want to tell me?"

Casey was completely caught off guard by the question, and her mind was suddenly racing. "What do you mean?"

"Last week," he said. "Did something happen last week?"

She quickly thought back to last week. Her conversation with Candy about what to do about Ben, going to his track practice, their first date. That was it. The rest was all normal everyday stuff. "I…I don't think so."

"It's okay, Casey. It's not a big deal."

*Did he talk to Candy or Nikki maybe? Did they say something to him?*

"Well," Casey started. But as she began to speak, this huge grin rushed over his face, and she stopped.

"Oh. My. Gosh."

Ben was laughing now.

"You just made all of that up to see if I would say something? That's your little trick?"

"Technically I think it belongs to some guy named Forer, but yeah, that's it."

"I meant *tell* me how you got her to give up a secret. Not *show* me…"

"Hey, I could have kept going…"

"And you *could* never get a third date…" she teased.

"Speaking of that. What night are you free to fulfill our little bet."

Casey stepped close to Ben and put her hands on his waist again. This time tucking them just slightly below the top hem of his jeans until her fingers brushed against his skin. She leaned up and kissed him slowly, teasing his lips. She moved down, leaving traces of her lips along his jaw line and neck.

His body tightened against her as both of his hands wrapped around her wrists. "How about," she said between kisses, "we just…forget…about that."

For a moment Ben didn't respond. He couldn't respond. His entire body felt warm, except for each and every place

Casey's lips touched his neck. He was trying to build his resolve, but the next kiss pushed him over the edge.

Ben moved his hands from her wrists to her waist and stepped closer to her until his body was pressed against hers. He pushed her against the front door and lifted her up as he kissed her. She wrapped her legs around his waist, and her hands around the back of his neck.

They kissed for several seconds and then Casey leaned her head back against the door and smiled. Ben let her slide back down to her feet and she looked up at him. "I'll take that as a yes."

# 34

## FOCUSED

*April 14, 2015*

The next day at work Casey found it hard to stay focused. If their first kiss was amazing, then she didn't think there were words that described how Ben had kissed her last night. Still, she was about to try.

It was just past 9 p.m. when Emma finally fell asleep. After a thirteen hour shift all Casey wanted to do was sleep, but Nikki was sitting excitedly on her couch with a bowl of popcorn and two glasses filled with Twin Springs Sweet Red Wine.

Nikki tapped on the empty couch cushion next to where she was sitting.

Casey rolled her eyes as she grabbed the glass of wine and sat down next to Nikki. She took two sips and rubbed her neck as she curled her legs up under her and leaned back against the couch.

"Okay, spill."

Casey looked back towards Emma's room and then over to Nikki. "Let's go to my room."

Nikki's eyes lit up. "Oh my gosh. You didn't."

Casey picked up the bowl of popcorn and walked towards her bedroom with Nikki following close behind. "Didn't what?"

"You slept with him on your second date," Nikki said.

Casey shut the door to her bedroom behind them. "What! No!"

Nikki looked around confused. "Then why are we in here with the door shut?"

"Did you forget there is a five year old girl asleep in the room down the hall?"

"So, you didn't sleep with him?"

"No!"

Nikki sat her glass on the nightstand and laid down on Casey's bed. "Well, that's a let down."

Casey bit her bottom lip.

"Wait, did you really, but you just don't want to say it out loud because of Emma?" Nikki whispered. "Okay, blink twice if you slept with him."

Casey stared blankly at Nikki.

"You're killing me," Nikki said. "Can you just tell me what happened?"

Casey hesitated. "He picked me up."

"He picked you up? Like in his car?"

"No. Like he physically picked me up."

"Casey, I love you, but I have no clue what you're talking about."

Casey sat down on the bed next to Nikki, her left leg folded under her and her right leg hanging off the side. She breathed in deeply. "We were standing at the front door and I was saying goodbye to Ben. We started kissing and the next thing I know my back is against the door, my legs are wrapped around his waist, and his tongue, oh my gosh." Casey breathed out deeply. "I've never been kissed like that in my entire life."

Nikki looked at Casey, but didn't say a word.

"What?" Casey said. "Is that bad?"

"That is the hottest thing I've ever heard."

# 35

## WHEN HE RUNS

*April 18, 2015*

Four days later and Casey still couldn't stop smiling as she walked up the bleacher stairs, each step echoing through the aluminum truss below her. Emma's left hand was wrapped around several of Casey's fingers, while her right was busy holding two scoops of vanilla ice cream in an old-fashioned wafer cone.

This was the last home meet of the season, and the stadium was absolutely packed. It was the only thing Ben had talked about all week long. Next weekend was their last away meet at LSU, three weeks after that were the Southeastern Conference Championships, and four weeks after that was the NCAA Championship. The schedule was pretty much burned into her head considering how long Ben spent talking about each race. At first it seemed as though he may just be talking off his nerves, but then Casey realized this wasn't nerves at all. This was something that was completely and utterly consuming him, and it kind of scared her in some sense.

Casey and Emma finally found a seat at the top of the bleachers just below a huge banner reading "Tom Jones Memorial Invitational." Casey had no idea who Tom Jones was, but she assumed pretty much no one else did either.

As they sat down, she scanned the field for Ben. Even though she'd been working twelve to fifteen hour days all week, they still managed to see each other or talk every day except Friday.

On Tuesday Casey got stuck at the hospital because the next shift resident was an hour late. She hadn't heard from Ben all day, and was surprised when she got in bed to find her phone ringing through with a video call. She was in pajamas with no makeup and bags under eyes, and yet the first thing he said when she accepted the call was, "you're beautiful." It wasn't just what he said though, it was the smile he said it with.

Wednesday night he came over for dinner and she made her world famous macaroni and cheese, which was really just macaroni noodles, cheese, butter, and milk. It was Emma's favorite though, and the blue flower he brought her made it unforgettable.

They didn't see each other on Thursday, because she got called back in to the hospital. But he texted her in the middle of the night, which was only a few hours into her shift. Fifteen minutes later she had found herself hiding in the break room, having the hottest text conversation she'd ever had.

Casey started to feel guilty about that night and the thoughts she was having right now. Not counting 8 Seconds, even though he did kiss her that night, they'd only been on three dates and yet she was nervous what might happen when the opportunity came up for more than a kiss. Fortunately, or unfortunately, there hadn't been a lot of opportunity for them to be alone…yet.

Casey looked down at Emma, who was literally covered in ice cream. Lines of dried vanilla ran down her fingers and around her mouth. There was even some in her hair. Casey grabbed a brown paper napkin from her pocket and wiped away the ice cream clinging to her hair behind her ear.

"Look, Mom." Emma pointed towards the left side of the infield. "It's Ben, it's Ben," she said, nearly dropping what was left of her ice cream.

Casey looked up to see Ben walking along side Parker. They were both wearing all blue. Blue tank tops with the word "Florida" in white writing on the center, blue breakaway sweat pants half buttoned down the sides, and even blue Nike sandals.

They walked across the infield for a few minutes, talking, and then Ben split away from Parker. He pulled his sweat pants off, revealing a pair of blue nylon shorts that she had seen on him before, and set them on top of a duffel bag. And then he slipped his sandals off and walked along the infield grass flexing his feet and ankles.

After several minutes Ben sat down next to his duffel bag and pulled out a pair of blue Nike shoes. He bent them each twice in his hand revealing a layer of thick black rubber under the minimalist running shoe. Then he slowly slipped them on and laced them up. The way he examined the laces reminded Casey of how she was taught to examine patients, never letting a single detail go unmissed.

She watched him stretch out and loosen up for the next ten minutes, while also trying to will him to look up at her. She had worn a pair of khaki capris with a drawstring at the bottom and a light blue tank top with spaghetti string straps that was probably a little too revealing, but that was the whole point.

He never looked up towards the stands, though. Not once.

The loudspeaker boomed overhead calling attention to all the runners participating in the 5000 meter. Casey watched as all the runners began to line up. Just beyond them she noticed the scoreboard change. In the upper left hand corner it read:

> *Event: 21 Heat: 1*

And just below that:

> *Lane 1: Collins, UF*
> *Lane 2, Morrie, FAMU*
> *Lane 3: Wilder, UF*
> *Lane 4: Zwiacz, TAMPA*
> *Lane 5: Swartz, TAMPA*
> *Lane 6: Fuentes, FIU*
> *Lane 7: Fellows, N. FLORIDA*
> *Lane 8: Sanders, UF*
> *Lane 9: Blunden, N. FLORIDA*
> *Lane 10: Gomes, FIU*

Casey looked back down to lane three where Ben was standing. She saw him look over to Parker, and Parker nodded.

The starter gun was louder than she anticipated and she blinked involuntarily. But after that Casey never took her eyes off Ben again.

Casey could hear Ben's voice in her head as they ran. "The 5000 meter race is just over three miles, which equates to twelve laps around the track." The first few laps mean nothing. Everyone is just settling in, trying to figure out if their pre-race strategy is actually going to work. Can they sit back, can they break from the pack early, can they get to the inside, and so on."

Ben had settled towards the middle of the pack, directly behind Parker.

"Laps four through eight are what Parker and I like to call the girl fight. It's literally like a bunch of girls poking, elbowing, and kicking their way into position. This part of the race takes a lot of patience."

Casey watched as all the runners crossed over into seven. She wondered what Ben thought about in those middle laps when he's alone out there on the track.

"Lap ten is where the fun begins. At this point there are only three laps left. Leaving the pack too early or too late could cost you the race. You've got to know not only the pace of the pack, but just how much you have left in the tank."

Towards the end of lap ten Ben made his first move. Parker pushed his way one lane to the left and Ben ran up the inside to the leading pack of three that was now four.

"Lap eleven is the toughest lap of the race. Everyone thinks the last lap wins the race, and that may be so, but the hardest lap is the second to last. During the final lap you'll have enough energy for one, maybe two moves if you're lucky. So lap eleven is the setup lap. You have to set yourself up to win the race in lap eleven."

Ben and a runner from North Florida were stride for stride behind the leader going into lap twelve. Parker was in another group of three battling for fourth, and the rest were about ten feet behind.

"Lap eleven is the magic lap. I know I said that you only have enough energy and time for one, maybe two moves. But the truth is anything can happen in the final lap."

At the first turn of the final lap everything changed. One of the guys running besides Parker made a push towards the front, passing Ben on the inside and running stride for stride with the same runner who led the entire race.

For a moment Casey thought that was it. This is how it was going to end. Ben was going to end up third and she was a bad luck charm.

That's when the magic began. Ben moved towards the outside lane, running alongside the two leaders. For a moment he didn't make another move, and it just looked like he was happy to be free from being trapped behind the entire race. Then he took off.

By the halfway mark he was matching the leaders stride for stride. At turn three he passed the leader and tucked back into the inside lane. By turn four all Casey saw was Ben. He was ten feet or more in front of the second and third place runners, but he didn't relent.

With each step he was picking up speed. His quads flexed forcefully above his knee each time his foot hit the track, and his arms pumped fiercely, cutting through the wind in front of him.

The crowd was chanting his name. "Ben-son! Ben-son! Ben-son!" Feet were pounding in unison on the bleachers and hands were shaking the fence down below.

People were looking from the runners, to the scoreboard, and back to the runners wondering if Benson Wilder would break another record. But Casey was only looking at one thing: his eyes.

They were locked on something distant. Something beyond the finish. Something he was trying to barrel through like a freight train with no passenger stops, only concerned with the final destination. It was a look Casey had never seen from Ben before. A look that scared her.

Ben crossed the finish line seconds later and it all ended just as fast as it had begun. He came to a stop at about the midpoint of the bleachers directly in line with where she was sitting, bent over and rested his hands on his knees. She watched the incessant rise and fall of his chest and back as he gasped for air.

Then he looked up at her and the only thing she could think is it felt like he was one person with her and an entirely different person when he runs.

# 36

## SECRETS

*April 18, 2015*

After the race Casey and Emma waited outside the front doors of the athletic facility for Ben. Emma climbed up on the silver tube railing and Casey stood behind her, making sure she didn't fall.

A few minutes later Ben walked through the doors, wearing a pair of longer mesh blue shorts, a gray UF Track & Field tank top, and a different pair of blue Nike shoes.

He started to walk over to them, but before he could move a slender brunette woman called his name. "Ben."

Ben turned around blocking the woman's view from Casey. "I told you, not now."

Casey couldn't see the woman's face from where she was standing, but she could hear the frustration in the woman's voice. "Ben I've given you as much time as I can. The story is running on Sunday, with or without your comment."

Ben stared at the lady for a moment, but didn't say another word. As he turned to walk towards Casey the woman glanced her way, and then over to Emma. She pulled her phone out of her pocket, typed something quickly, and of all things took a picture of Ben walking away. Then she pulled open the door and disappeared.

Before Casey could say anything, Emma blurted out, "Did you win?"

Casey smiled, "Honey, we just watched him win."

"I know," Emma said. "But I just wanted to make sure."

Ben strained a smile and Casey knew something was wrong. "I did win," he said with a wink.

"Can we go play on the field?" Emma asked.

Casey looked up at Ben and back to Emma. "Maybe next time," she said.

"But mom, you said—" Emma pouted.

"Emma," Casey said, silencing her.


They started walking down the concrete ramp towards the parking lot. Emma walked several feet ahead, tapping the metal railing as she hummed to herself.

"Thanks for coming," Ben said.

"And miss a chance to see the great Benson Wilder?" Casey joked.

Ben tried to smile, but it came across as more of a grimace to Casey.

When they reached the parking lot, Casey walked over to the passenger side and unlocked the door for Emma. After she sat down, she reached across and pulled her seat belt across her. "I'm going to go say goodbye to Mr. Ben. You sit right here, okay?" Casey pulled out her phone and handed it to Emma. "You can play Angry Birds if you want."

"Can I play Panda Pop?" Emma said excitedly?

Casey kissed Emma on the forehead. "You sure can."

Casey left the door open halfway and walked over to Ben, who was leaning against the back of his truck. She noticed his demeanor had eased a bit not bothering to hide the fact that his eyes were clinging tightly to her body moving up from the hemline of her capris. They left her waist and moved over her blouse as it slinked against her skin in the wind. She knew that Emma might be watching so she had to be careful, but she wanted to try and cheer up whatever was bothering Ben.

When she was within a few feet, Ben pushed off the back of the truck. She stepped her right leg between both of his, however, forcing him back against it. His hands instinctively went to her waist as she pressed her lips against his. She opened her mouth slightly and for a split second let his tongue play with hers.

She wanted more than a goodbye kiss. She wanted him to unlatch the tailgate and lift her up on it. She wanted to wrap her legs around his waist and run her fingers through his hair as he kissed softly down her neck. Her heart was already racing, but she would have to wait for all of that.

She pressed both of her hands against his chest and spun away so that they were both leaning their backs against the truck side by side.

"Wow," Ben whispered, slightly dazed by what just happened. He turned around and leaned his elbows against the top rail of the truck bed and lifted his foot to rest on the back tire.

"Please don't take this the wrong way," he started.

Casey's smile faded. That was not exactly the response she wanted to hear. Did she just do something wrong? Her mind was already jumping to a hundred different conclusions. *Who starts a sentence like that? Of course I'm going to take it the wrong way now.*

"I can't see you for a little bit."

Casey's thoughts raced back to the woman that had followed Ben out of the locker room, and to just before that when he finished the race. Something had been off with him since she first saw him today, but she didn't say anything. She just stood there.

"Just for a week," he said, quickly turning to face her. "Final exams are this week, and our last meet before regionals is next Saturday."

Ben grabbed both of her hands and pulled her back in front of him. "I want to see you more than anything, but I can't afford to be here without my scholarship, so I have to make sure my finals go well. And Coach gave us a big speech about not losing focus now that the season is almost over. Spring semester ends in a week and the break in our normal routine before regionals can be serious if we don't stay focused. I just need to get through this week, and then I promise I'll make it up to you."

What Ben said made sense. Casey could remember back to final exams, and they sucked. And she could understand his need to focus. That's not what bothered her. What bothered her is that when she looked back at him, he still had the same look as before. Like he was telling her the truth, just not the full truth.

Casey thought about it for a moment and regardless of whether or not this was a good time to ask, she asked anyways. "What aren't you telling me?"

Ben looked down as he ran his thumbs over the back of her hands. She could feel the subtle callouses move nervously across her skin.

Casey squeezed his hands lightly. "Ben," she said. "What is it? Is it something to do with that lady after the race?"

He didn't respond.

"Did I do something?" Casey asked.

"No," Ben said immediately. "You," he said looking up at her, "are perfect."

"Then what? I know you're keeping something from me. It's not just from today. Ever since the first time we went out you've held some part of yourself back. I pushed it aside thinking you'd tell me when you're ready. But…"

"I want to tell you, Casey."

"Then tell me."

Ben breathed in deeply and exhaled. "That lady you saw earlier. She's a journalist. She wants to do a piece on me."

Casey didn't understand. "Okay, isn't that good?"

Ben looked over to the car where Emma was sitting. "It's not just about me."

Casey smiled, "Don't tell me they're going to include Parker."

"No," Ben said. "Amanda and Grace."

Casey thought about the names for a minute, but they didn't ring a bell. "Are they on the track team?"

Ben shook his head no. He barely got the next words out. "They were my wife and daughter."

# 37

## Too Hard

*April 22, 2015*

It was Wednesday afternoon and practice had just ended. Ben sat in Coach Melvick's office with a towel around his neck. Sweat was still dripping off him turning parts of the chair a darker shade of blue.

"Do you remember the conversation we had when you first got here?" Coach Melvick said.

Ben thought back to last August. He remembered the conversation like it was yesterday, but he didn't respond to Coach.

"I told you if I ever thought you couldn't handle this I'd yank your ass off this team quicker than a chicken on a June Bug."

Ben was trying to think if he had ever seen any of Uncle Jim's chickens eat a June Bug, but Coach continued.

"You know who called me, *at my home,* on Sunday after that damn article was published?"

Ben shook his head no, not sure if he was supposed to respond or just keep listening to Coach.

"Your girlfriend."

"My girlfriend?" Ben said confused.

"Yes, the Athletic Director called and wanted to make sure Benson Wilder was okay because we couldn't afford to have one of our star athletes 'emotionally unstable.'"

Ben couldn't help but smile. "I'm fine Coach."

"And that's exactly what I told him. But you wouldn't believe the darndest thing happened a couple days later. I got another call from your girlfriend. Only this time he didn't lecture me on the "emotional stability" of my athletes. He lectured me on their eligibility to compete. Apparently Mr. Benson Wilder has been spotted training at the break of fucking dawn in addition to our regularly scheduled practices and workouts. Possibly breaking NCAA in-season training rules."

"Coach…" Benson started.

Coach held up his hand. "Save it. You're done until the meet on Saturday."

"But Coach I'm just trying to stay focused."

"Well tomorrow and Friday you can stay focused in your dorm room, because if you show up to practice you're off the team."

"But Coach…"

Coach didn't say a word. Instead he just pointed towards the door. Ben stood up and wiped the sweat off the chair he had been sitting in.

"Ben."

Ben opened the door and turned around to face Coach before leaving. He looked back at the old man, his blue polo shirt tucked into his khaki pants, and his gray flattop. Coach didn't say another word, but Ben knew what he was thinking. "I'm fine Coach. I promise."

# 38

## Temptation

*April 22, 2015*

"I can't believe you haven't talked to him since," Nikki said. "How long has it been now?"

Casey turned over on her side, her combed cotton bed sheets stretching softly against her. She looked at the clock on her night stand. "Four days, four hours, and about twenty minutes."

"Okay, tell me how you left it again."

"He said he needed a week to focus on finals because he couldn't afford to lose his scholarship. I could tell something else was wrong, so I pressed him."

"And that's when he told you his wife died giving birth to his daughter, and his daughter died to medical complications years later?" Nikki asked.

"Yes," Casey said.

"And what did you say?"

"I didn't say anything. I just hugged him."

"Have you seen the segment they did on him?"

163

"No, I want to hear it from him, not from some reporter on television."

"I don't know if you want to hear this but everybody has been talking about it on campus," Nikki said.

Casey didn't say anything.

"Okay, well it's Wednesday now. The week is halfway over. You said you're going to see him on Sunday when he gets back from LSU?"

"Yeah, but…" Casey started.

"But what?" Nikki asked.

"But what if things are different between us?"

"Do you want them to be different?"

"No," Casey said.

"Then when you see him don't let them be different."

"You sure you don't mind watching Emma on Sunday?"

"Do we have to go over this every single time I watch Emma?"

"I'm sorry," Casey said. "I just—"

"Stop it. I love watching Emma. If you ever ask me and I can't, I'll tell you."

"Okay," Casey said. "I guess I'm going to try and get some sleep."

"Okay, I'll call you tomorrow," Nikki said.

Casey plugged her phone in and sat it by her pillow on the edge of the bed. She rolled over and looked up at the ceiling. Little strips of moonlight crawled across the random textures. The image of Ben leaning against his truck as they drove away that day after the race was still ingrained in her mind.

Everything he said that day made sense. He needed to focus on finals and the last regular season meet at LSU this weekend. The spring semester ended tomorrow and most students would be spending their summer at the beach, while Ben was busy training for regionals and barring any unforeseen circumstances the NCAA Championships.

His coach was right, the last thing he needed was to lose focus and screw something up school related or perform terrible at LSU and put his team in a bad situation for regionals.

She pressed the round white circle at the bottom of her iPhone one more time. It was 10:43 p.m., exactly seventy-three minutes past her self-imposed bedtime.

*Maybe I should just call him. He's probably not even asleep yet. Maybe he's lying in bed looking at his phone every other minute too.*

Casey swiped the lock screen to the right and pressed the little green phone icon on the bottom left of the screen. She scrolled through her contacts until she got to his name. *I'm just going to call him.*

Instead she rolled over and put the phone on her nightstand and then rolled back onto her back. *Or I'll just stare at the ceiling for another hour.*

It didn't take an hour though, only another ten minutes before she started to fall asleep. When it came to staying up late, she was a lightweight.

*Tnnnnt.*

*Tnnnth.*

Casey turned in her sleep. The sound at the window had pulled her into that half asleep, half-awake state, but she ignored it.

*Tnntt. Tnt.*

Her eyes opened. There it was again. She looked over at the window. The white sheer curtains were drawn, but not fully. There was a one-foot vertical sliver of the window she could see out. An old maple tree sat outside her window and some of the branches rubbed against the roof on windy nights. Sometimes it would wake her up, but it was strangely peaceful.

*Tnnnt. Tnnnt.*

She heard the sound again. She knew it wasn't coming from the maple tree. Not because she was some kind of weird nature sound expert, but because she just saw two brown twigs bounce off her window, followed by two more.

Casey pulled the blanket off and stepped out of bed. As soon as she got to the window, she knew exactly what the sound was. Crouched in the same bright blue tank top he always wore was Ben.

She undid the latch on the window, lifted it open and bent over to look out. Before she could say anything, Ben started to climb in through the window.

*Is this really happening? Is my boyfriend sneaking in through my window in the middle of the night?*

My boyfriend? She realized that was the first time she'd referred to Ben as her boyfriend. She almost felt sixteen again.

Casey closed the window behind Ben. "What are you doing?" she whispered.

Without hesitation Ben ran his hand along her face until it cupped the back of her neck. He looked down at her and pressed his forehead against hers bringing his lips so close to hers that with each breath they barely brushed against one another.

"Ben," she whispered. "I thought you needed to…" Her words trailed off as he gently pressed his lips against hers. It felt like a feather running across her lips, softer than she'd ever been kissed before.

166

She had two immediate thoughts: *Oh my gosh* and *what if my breath stinks.*

His lips left hers and started to move deliberately across her face. He started with the corner of her mouth and then just below her cheekbone. She could feel his breath exhale unhurriedly against her skin and the slight coarseness of his face as his lips traced along her jawbone.

Casey's hands moved to his arms and she breathed out his name faintly. "Ben…"

She felt him close in on the bottom of her left ear, his teeth lightly pulling down on her ear lobe until she could feel tens of thousands of nerve endings explode.

Her right hand moved over his shoulder and to the back of his neck, scratching just below his hair, as his tongue continued to kiss and flick in the small space behind her ear.

She let out a weak sigh the moment his lips touched her neck and any thoughts she had left vanished.

His hands wrapped around her bare shoulders as his lips kept moving further down her body. First across her collarbone and then down her chest until his lips reached the upper fabric of her shirt.

All of Casey wanted to lift her shirt over her head and make him keep going, but she couldn't move. His hand slid from her shoulders, brushing delicately against the sides of her chest until they stopped on her waist as he went to his knees.

She watched his head sink slowly below her and ran her fingers through his hair. He lifted the hem of her shirt just slightly to kiss along the waistline of her shorts. Her head fell back as she breathed heavily and she felt herself lift up slightly on her toes, revealing even more of herself to him.

Casey's hands moved to the top of his, holding them tightly against her and when he looked up at her she could see the desire in his eyes.

Ben pulled his hands from hers and ran his fingertips just inside the cusp of her shorts. He pulled at them lightly and another shock wave of nerve endings erupted as his lips moved across the top of her panties.

Even through the cotton of her shorts she could feel his hands as they moved down her legs. His lips followed behind them brushing against her upper thigh and started to move inwards to places she's never been kissed before.

Ben moved his hands down the backside of her calves as he continued kissing every inch of her thigh. The whole room felt like it was slowly spinning, and Casey didn't know if she could stand much longer.

"Ben," she whispered, her heart racing.

Ben stood up at the sound of her voice and stared at her lips as they said his name again: "Ben." But he didn't respond.

His hands moved back to her waist and he began to push her backward slowly until the back of her legs felt the cool metal of the bed frame.

He laid her down against the bed and followed, lying next to her, only to start all over again.

His face hovered over hers, kissing the side of her head and her cheek, leaving traces of his lips everywhere but on hers. She could feel his wet tongue approach her ear again, licking and teasing.

Her body shuddered against his and it was all she could do to hold back the soft moans and groans she wanted so badly to release.

Casey opened her eyes for what felt like the first time in hours and realized her hands had been on his chest this whole time. The second she moved them to his waist she could feel chills glide across his body. She started to move her hand lower against his skin and his arms gave way, dropping his weight onto her.

She finally let out a soft moan as their bodies started to move together. His lips found hers again and she instinctively found herself wanting to pull his shirt off him. At that moment all of her thoughts returned and suddenly she was terrified at what was about to happen.

"Ben," she said into his lips. Casey knew if she didn't stop him now she wouldn't be able to stop in a second. "Ben, we can't," Casey said again between kisses. Her body betrayed her words though as she raised her legs against his sides bringing him inexplicably closer.

"I know," Ben said. But he didn't stop. His tongue pressed into hers and she welcomed it. Her hands began to pull his shirt up just slightly and she could feel his bare stomach against hers.

He moved away from her lips and back to her neck, and her back arched as his hips moved against hers. Casey opened her eyes and looked back up at the same empty ceiling she was staring at before he showed up, and gently pushed him towards it.

Ben rose up on his arms, hovering over her, and she smiled as his hungry blue eyes burned into hers. Then she did something she knew she shouldn't have done. She ran her tongue over the bottom of her lip.

He lowered himself closer to her again, but she stopped him.

Not taking his eyes off her he collapsed to the bed beside her. "I'm sorry. I've just been thinking about you non-stop all week. I thought I could just see you for a second, but when I got here…I couldn't…everything about you is just…"

"Just what?"

"Perfect. Which is why I can't be in this room another second with you, or I won't ever be able to stop again." Ben leaned down and kissed Casey on the cheek one last time, and she could feel his reluctance in leaving.

She watched him stand up and walk over to the window, still not taking his eyes off her. Then he shook his head with a smile, and climbed out the window, pulling it shut behind him.

# 39

## With You

*April 26, 2015*

Casey shut the car door behind her and pressed the garage door button to close on her way inside. Emma followed behind her as Casey bumped the coffee table with her shin.

"Shi—oot!" she yelled.

She grabbed the remote and clicked through the channels looking for the SEC Network.

"Mom," Emma said from the kitchen. "Can I have some cookies before dinner?"

"Sure honey," Casey said, not even hearing the question.

By the time she found the right channel just over one lap remained. The camera zoomed in on Ben and two other runners as they crossed into the final lap. The camera zoomed back out revealing a small gap between the rest of the runners. Casey couldn't make out the faces but there were two other blue Florida shirts in the mix, and she knew one must be Parker.

Emma sat down in the arm chair next to her, but Casey didn't even notice the plate of Oreos.

After the first turn of the final lap the lead runner picked up the pace. Ben followed suit and the top three runners ran the backstretch in a single file line, with Ben now in second. At turn three nothing changed, and then at turn four still nothing.

"Why isn't he making his move?" Casey said out loud.

Casey's heart was pounding. They pulled within several hundred feet of the finish line, but Ben still sat in second place.

"Only two hundred feet now separate Blake Anthony from pulling off a huge upset over Ben Wilder," the announcer said.

Casey's hands squeezed around the remote until the plastic started to groan.

"Wait," the other announcer said. "Look at this."

Ben darted out from behind the leader and pulled up alongside him, each step in unison. The camera zoomed in on the finish and Casey watched as Ben crossed the finish line one step ahead.

"Unbelievable," the announcer said. "Benson Wilder, the current SEC record holder, will head to regionals in a few weeks unbeaten."

* * *

Just over twenty four hours later Casey pulled into the parking lot in front of Ben's dorm. She wanted to do something special with him tonight. Not just because she hadn't seen him in a few days, but also because after his win on Saturday he was officially going into the SEC Regionals as the number one ranked runner in the 5000 meter for the SEC and the number two ranked runner in the nation.

The problem was that not a lot of places were open on Sunday night, especially since she ended up working two hours past her normal shift. It was just a few minutes past eight when she picked up her phone to call him. Before she could dial, though, he came walking out the front door.

She was so used to seeing him in blue running shorts, or blue sweats, or basically any of the blue and white or gray athletic gear the university supplied. He wasn't wearing any of that. Not even the running shoes.

He looked the same way he did on their first date. He was wearing jeans and a collared pull-over with the sleeves rolled up that had thick red and navy horizontal stripes. He also had on a pair of brown boots, and a thick brown belt. He looked at ease as he walked towards her.

Casey suddenly got worried right before Ben opened the passenger side door. She thought back to what Nikki had said to her. *If you don't want things to be different, don't let them be different.*

All of her worries were erased the second he stepped into the car. Because the very first thing he did was to hold her face in his hand and pull her lips into his. "I missed you," he said.

"I missed you too."

He kissed her again. "If you want," and again, "we can just," and again, "stay," and again, "right," and again, "here." Her mouth moved in sync with his and she thought back to Wednesday night when his lips had moved effortless across her body.

A car behind them honked and they both looked around. She was still parked illegally, blocking one side of the road. "Or not," he laughed.

She put the car in drive and looped around the complex and back out of the parking lot. They drove down fraternity row, which was surprisingly quiet, even for a Sunday. And then turned on Museum Road which took them past Lake Alice and the wedding chapel. Across the lake and in the distance Casey could see the blue lights from the helipad on top of the Children's Hospital, and that gave her an idea. "What's your favorite fast food?"

"Fast food? I think it's illegal or something for doctors to eat fast food," he joked.

Casey looked over at Ben, still waiting for an answer.

"You're serious?" he asked." Okay, well if you must know. Zaxby's. Fried chicken fingers, crinkle fries, Texas toast, and honey mustard drizzled over it all."

Casey could picture the sign above Zaxby's with bright neon lights and a giant rooster. Maybe it was the words honey mustard and drizzle, or just the fact that she hadn't eaten since before noon, but it sounded amazing.

They pulled into the drive-in a few minutes later and Casey scanned the starlit menu. The salad looked amazing. Actually pretty much every image of food looked amazing, but Casey opted to get the exact same thing as Ben.

When they pulled out of Zaxby's, Casey turned left onto Archer back the same way they came until she pulled into a turn lane just past Shands Hospital.

When the light turned green, Casey made a left in front of the hospital, then a right into a large parking garage across the street.

"I saw this movie once where this girl took her boyfriend to an abandoned parking garage, and then chopped him up into little pieces…"

Casey drove up several ramps until she reached the top floor of the garage and then parked on the far end. She opened the sunroof and turned the car off. When she looked up, it felt as though there wasn't a single cloud for miles. Thousands of bright white lights stared back at her.

"Wow," Ben said.

"I come up here sometimes on break when I work the night shift. Sometimes it's just a dark black sky, but tonight it really is amazing."

For the next ten minutes they both sat there and ate. Casey asked Ben about what it's like to travel to meets and to race in different places all over the U.S.

Ben dipped his Texas toast into some honey mustard and took a bite. "I don't know. I mean we're mostly just in the southeast. Kentucky, Arkansas, Virginia, North Carolina, Louisiana. We got to go to Philadelphia for the Penn Relays, which was kind of neat, and out to California for the Trojan Invitational. But the SEC Championships are back in Alabama in a few weeks. But," he paused and looked over at her. "The one place I do want to see is Hayward Field."

"Where's that?"

"University of Oregon. Home of Nike and Steve Prefontaine."

Casey finished her last chicken tender and Ben tossed her plate in the bag that was now just trash. "Do you ever get tired of it?" she said.

"Tired of all the travel?"

"No, I mean, tired of running."

"Right now I don't know what I would do without running," Ben said.

"What do you mean?"

"Nothing. I mean, not nothing, but…"

"But what?"

"It's hard to explain."

"Will you try?"

"Well. Let me ask you a question."

"Okay."

"You know when you have a feeling or memory that you don't want to fade away, but you don't' know how to keep it?"

"Of course," Casey said.

"That feeling comes back when I run, if only for 13 minutes."

Ben didn't say anything for a minute and they both sat there just staring back up at the stars. Casey couldn't help but wonder if the memory he was talking about was of his daughter. She turned on her side, her elbow resting against the seat back, and looked over at Ben. "You remember that night when you told me what you were thinking?"

"You mean the night you first kissed me?"

"You kissed me!"

Ben laughed. "Yes, I remember that night. Why?"

Casey reached over with her left hand and placed it on top of his. "Will you tell me what you're thinking again?"

"I don't know. That was kind of a one-time-only thing."

"What happened to I can ask you anything?"

"You can, but," he said. "You've got to have the password."

Casey raised her eyebrows and moved as close as she could until her body pushed up against the center console. She bit her bottom lip, and then leaned in and kissed him. She let her lips linger softly on his for a moment and then pulled away. "Was that the right password?"

Ben's right hand moved out from under hers and found the soft cloth of her light blue scrubs pressed tightly against her leg. "That was definitely the first part." He squeezed her leg gently.

Casey slid over the console until she was straddling Ben. Looking down at him she saw a flicker of surprise in his eyes, and to be honest, she was a little surprised too. "How about now?" she said.

"You're getting closer."

She lowered her weight from her knees onto his lap. She moved one hand to his shoulder while the other slowly glided up and down his arm as she leaned over just inches from his face. "Close enough?"

His hands started to slide up her legs towards her waist, but she stopped him. She sat up enough to grab his wrists and folded his hands against his chest. Then she repeated, "What are you thinking?"

"What *am* I thinking, or what *was* I thinking?"

She smiled. "Both."

Ben took a deep breath and let it out slowly. "I was thinking about giving up…"

Casey's hands wrapped tighter around Ben's wrists as she pushed them into this chest. "You can't give up!"

"Let me finish," he said. "I was thinking about if I have ever given up. Not just as a runner, but as a person. And I was thinking those might now be one and the same thing."

"What else?"

Ben laughed. "If Little Miss Impatient would stop interrupting, then I might be able to finish."

*Sorry,* she mouthed with a little bit of sass.

"I was also thinking about how I could eat Zaxby's literally every day. And how I don't like shoelaces, especially long ones that you can step on. And wondering what fresh air smells like and if I've ever smelled it. And whether or not it's sad that we never truly see the stars, only the light they shined years and years ago, and how similar our lives can sometimes be."

Casey started to say something, but Ben went on. "That's what I *was* thinking. But now I'm only thinking about you." He removed her hands from his wrists and wrapped them just above her elbows and pulled her closer.

Her hands pressed against his chest and she could feel her heart beating faster.

He moved his hands lightly over her arms, to her shoulders and down her back giving her goosebumps. "I'm thinking about the subtle curves of your body from your legs all the way up to your lips." She tried to stop from shaking, but she couldn't as he pressed into the small of her back and ran his fingers up towards her shoulders again.

He slid his hands back down to her waist and wrapped them around her until his thumbs were just subtly pressing into the top of her thigh. "I'm thinking about how I love the way you walk."

"I walk funny," Casey said, half smiling and half biting her bottom lip.

Ben moved his hands off her waist and over the top of her hands that were still pressing into his chest. "I'm thinking about how you seem happy and kind every time I'm with you, and how that makes me just want to never be apart. But mostly, I'm thinking about how perfectly you fit in my arms."

Casey leaned towards Ben and kissed him, then curled her head just below his neck and collapsed. His arms wrapped around her and she felt so emotionally drained. A single tear formed and she quickly wiped it away, hiding it from him.

"What was she like?" Casey said quietly.

"Who?"

"Your wife."

Ben took a deep breath, Casey's head moving with the rise and fall of his chest. As much as he had been trying to avoid it, he knew a question like this would eventually come. "She was…strong," he said.

He hesitated and Casey wanted to ask him how, but then he went on.

"When she got pregnant people blamed her. I had all these running scholarships, and they didn't understand when I gave it all up. So, they blamed her for it. My friends, her friends. Her family. No one wanted us to keep the baby. And when we got married, it got even worse.

"She was so steadfast through it all. And it made me love her even more. Contrary to what everyone thought we didn't get married because of Grace. We got married because we were in love. It was a young love, maybe even a foolish love, but it was a pure love.

"That didn't make it any easier though. She used to always say, 'It's going to be hard, but not impossible.'

Ben breathed in through his nose and his voice was shaky. "She was always strong."

# 40

## Handcuffs

*April 26, 2015*

Emma came running out of her room as soon as Casey and Ben stepped through the front door, still holding hands. "Mommy, Mommy."

"Yessy, yessy. Hmph, wow you are getting big," Casey said as she lifted Emma up and perched her against her right hip.

"Guess what?"

"What?"

"You're supposed to guess."

Casey looked back at Ben who was laughing quietly. "Okay, ummm, you grew a pair of wings and learned to fly."

"No, only birds can fly. Aunt Nikki taught me how to braid my hair, look." Emma pulled a thin braid that was tucked behind her right ear.

"Wow that is very pretty. Now go tell Aunt Nikki goodnight because she needs to get home to go to bed."

Nikki bent down to hug Emma. "Goodnight, Aunt Nikki."

"Goodnight sweetheart," Nikki said.

"Alright, now go get in bed and I'll be in in a minute to tuck you in."

"Can Mr. Ben tuck me in tonight?"

Both Nikki and Casey turned to look at Ben. In Casey's mind the entire world had stopped spinning, but before she could even say anything, Ben held out his hand towards Emma. "I would love to, but you have to lead the way or I might get lost."

Casey looked over to see if he was really okay with this, but Ben never looked up.

Instead Emma wrapped her tiny hands around two of Ben's fingers and started pulling him down the hall towards her room. "It's really not that hard to remember," Casey heard Emma say. "My room is the first door on the right, just past the kitchen. Plus my name is even on the door…" Their voices faded as they turned down the hall.

Casey stared silently towards the hallway.

"Are you okay?" Nikki asked.

"I don't know."

"Do you want—"

Casey interrupted her. "Am I a bad mom?"

"Casey. No. You're an incredible mom. Why would you even say that?"

Casey leaned back against the front door. "I just don't know what I'm even doing. I've been hanging out with Ben so much…and you've been watching Emma…"

"You know I never mind watching Emma. Of course, it would be nice if I could say no because I had a guy bringing *me* flowers and taking *me* to dinner, but I don't."

"It all feels like it's happening so fast."

Nikki laughed.

"How is this funny? I'm freaking out."

Nikki put her hands on Casey's shoulders. "Okay, I really need to put some things into perspective for you. You've been dating an incredibly attractive star athlete at a major university for almost a month. He probably has girls falling all over him and he is here choosing to be with you."

"Those girls don't have daughters, though," Casey said.

"That's the point. He could be out there with some cute little blonde with absolutely no strings attached. Instead, he just walked your little girl down the hall to tuck her in. So, just calm down, and enjoy the rest of your night with him. Can you do that?"

Casey was lost in thought.

Nikki snapped her fingers several times. "Hello? Earth to Casey."

"Yes, yes. I can do that."

"Okay, then go back there and tuck in your daughter with your amazing guy."

Casey took a deep breath and smiled. "Okay, I can do that."

"And later if he goes all Fifty Shades of Grey on you, I want all the details."

Casey's face went flush, as she thought back to last Wednesday night. "Do you think he's going to try something tonight?" she asked, unsure if she was nervous or excited.

Nikki laughed. "Oh my gosh girl. It was a joke. Just breathe. And call me later. And remember…you don't want the handcuffs too tight."

"I hate you," Casey said, smiling, just before she shut the door in Nikki's face.

Casey tiptoed down the hallway and stopped just short of Emma's door. It was wide open and the lamp light from her nightstand poured out into the hallway. Emma's bed sat just below the window on the wall opposite where Casey was, but she could still make out their voices clearly.

\* \* \*

"She does?" Ben said. "Well, I don't think you want to hear me sing, but…how about a story?"

Emma thought about it for a moment. "Okay."

"Okay, but first you have to get really comfortable."

Emma adjusted her pillow underneath her, and wrapped her arms tight around Tinker, her stuffed owl.

"Are you really comfortable now?" Ben asked.

"Mm-hhm."

"Are you really, really comfortable?"

Emma giggled. "Yes."

"Okay, good. Now, this is one of my favorite stories of all times. But I don't want you to just listen to it, I want you to picture it in your head. So, close your eyes and picture the biggest and coolest race track you've ever seen."

Emma squeezed her eyes shut.

"Can you see it?"

She nodded as she yawned.

"Okay. Once upon a time there was a little boy named Charlie. And Charlie was the fastest boy in the whole world. But one day Charlie was playing with his friends and…he fell down and broke his leg.

"Charlie went to the doctor and the doctor put a cast on his leg and told Charlie he would be just fine in a few months.

"Days went by, and weeks went by, and finally three months had passed and it was time for Charlie to get his cast taken off. So, he went to the doctor and the doctor took off his cast and said, 'Your leg is as good as new.'

"Charlie reached down and felt his leg and it felt kind of funny. He looked up at the doctor and asked, 'Will I be able to run just as fast as before?'

"The doctor looked at him with a great big smile and whispered in his ear, 'you will be even faster.'

"Now once a year there is a championship race between all the fastest boys in the world. Charlie began to practice for this race by running every day, but…he was still scared that if he tried to run really fast, he might break his leg again.

"The day of the big race came. It would be Charlie's first race since he broke his leg. All the fastest kids in the world were there, and Charlie had always been the fastest. Today was different though, because for the first time in his life Charlie doubted himself. Was he really the fastest still?"

Ben looked down at Emma, who was already sound asleep. He watched the steady rise and fall of her little chest, and wondered if she was dreaming about Charlie. He grabbed the blanket and pulled it up just a little higher, remembering just how much he missed this.

Then he reached over and quietly pulled the small brass chain on the lamp. The room went dark, except for the soft moonlight that crept in through the blinds.

He quietly got to his feet and walked backwards towards the door, making sure Emma didn't wake up. When he reached the hallway, he saw Casey sitting on the hallway floor with her back against the ground and her knees tucked to her chest.

Ben knelt down onto the cream colored plush carpet. It almost felt like grass when he pressed his hands against it and sat leaning against the wall next to Casey.

"Was he really the fastest still?" Casey asked.

Ben smiled and picked up the story where he left off. "All the kids began to gather around the starting line. Some were stretching, and others were talking, but Charlie was pacing nervously on the infield grass.

"He looked around and noticed some of the kids were pointing at him and whispering things. That's when he heard an unfamiliar crunch under his foot. He bent down and picked up a pair of glasses and brushed them off against his shorts. They were bent, but they weren't broken. He looked around to see who may have dropped them and that's when he saw her.

"She was the most beautiful girl he had ever seen, and for a moment all the world seemed to stop. He tried to pull his eyes away from her, but he couldn't. His world began to slowly spin as the girl moved towards him. His heart started racing like he was rounding the final turn of the race. And yet this girl seemed to be perfectly calm.

"'Thank you' the girl said. Charlie heard her, but he couldn't respond. His world was still suspended from all motion, except for the incessant beating of his heart.

"The girl spoke again, but he couldn't hear anything but the bright blue sound that was coming from her eyes. And as he ran that day, that's all he thought about."

Casey closed her eyes and leaned against his shoulder and thought all over again about the first day they met.

\* \* \*

A few minutes later and Ben followed Casey into the kitchen. He sat down at one of the countertop stools as she walked over to the pantry. "So, you never told me how final exams went."

"Right now I'm just glad they're over."

Casey opened up a cabinet and pulled out an electric tea kettle. She poured about two cups of tap water in, sat it on the counter and plugged it in. "I'm going to make a cup of mint tea. Do you want some?"

"Sure."

Casey leaned down resting her elbows on the counter across from Ben. "So, what are you going to do now that classes are over?"

"Coach has us on the same practice schedule until regionals in couple weeks. But…now that I'm going to have a little more free time I was thinking about hanging out with this one girl I kind of have a thing for."

"Oh really?" Casey said.

Ben got up and walked slowly around the bar counter towards Casey. "Yeah, she's a doctor. She's really smart, and fun, and has this absolutely gorgeous smile."

Casey turned around, her body leaning back against the counter as Ben moved closer to her. "She sounds pretty great. What did you plan to do with this girl with all this extra free time?"

Ben lowered his hands down to her waist and lifted Casey gently on top of the counter. He stepped close to her and she wrapped her bare feet around the backs of his legs. "There's a lot I want to do with this girl," he said. He brushed aside several strands of hair on her shoulder and leaned in pressing his lips softly against her check. "I thought I could take her to dinner one night." He ran his hands over her shoulders. "And take her to a movie."

"Mmm. I bet she would like that," Casey said. "What else?"

Ben ran his fingers over the back of her neck as his thumb cupped her face just in front of her ear.

Casey bent her neck back slightly looking up at him only inches away.

Ben leaned forward and kissed her. "I was thinking about taking her to get some ice cream." He kissed her again, but this time for a little longer. "Maybe go putt-putt golf," he said smiling. "Maybe just have a few lazy Sunday afternoons on the couch with her."

He started to speak again, but this time Casey stopped him. She tugged the bottom of his shirt pulling him back to her. His lips parted and she felt the warmth of his tongue against hers. Her legs tightened even more around his waist and his hands moved under her thighs lifting her off the counter. He started to carry her towards her bedroom, their lips never parting.

But just as he got to her door the tea kettle began to scream.

# 41

## RHYTHM

*May 10, 2015*

"Can we go play now?" Emma asked.

"Finish your vegetables first," Casey said.

Emma scooped up a spoonful of Lima beans and shoved them into her mouth and smiled.

Ben laughed and Casey shot him a playfully scolding look.

This had turned into an everyday occurrence for them over the past week. After work Casey would pick up Emma from daycare and find Ben waiting on her doorstep with a smile. Once he even picked her up when Casey got stuck at the hospital, and when she got home that night he had a warm plate of fried pork chops and mashed potatoes waiting.

Casey got up from the table, walked over to the hall closet and came back with two board games in her hand. "Okay, we've got Operation and Mouse Trap."

"Can we play doctor instead?"

"You don't want to play Operation," Casey asked again.

Emma shook her head.

Ben winked at Casey, "I'm always down to play doctor."

"Alright," Casey said. "But just remember you asked for it."

Ben cleared the table, while Casey cleaned the dishes, and Emma started preparing the "hospital," which was essentially the couch with a blanket spread out and a pillow on one end.

When they finished they found Emma sitting in a chair by the couch. "Okay, Mr. Ben is the patient. You're the doctor," Emma said pointing to Casey. "And I'm the nurse."

"How do we play?" Ben asked.

Emma tapped on the couch. "You lie down here, and we fix you."

Casey looked at Ben. "We might be here all night," she joked.

Ben winked at Casey again. "That's fine. I can go all night."

Casey looked down at Emma who was shuffling through a homemade first aid kit that contained mostly Band-Aids, gauze, and hair ties. Luckily she was completely oblivious to Ben's comment. *Stooopp,* Casey mouthed.

Ben grinned and pinched Casey's leg.

Emma pulled out a couple Band-Aids, a pink hair tie, and a roll of gauze. "Okay, I will fix his hand and head wounds. You have to check his chest and legs. Do you have your skesosope?"

"Steth-o-scope," Casey corrected. "And where is the one I gave you?"

Emma opened up her little black bag. "I forgot I even put it in here." She pulled out the black and silver stethoscope and handed it to Casey. Then she grabbed Ben's hand and began wrapping the hair tie around two of his fingers. "Your fingers are broken, so we've got to make a splint."

Ben looked down at his fingers. "That's a very pretty splint. My fingers already feel better."

"No, you can't move," Emma said. "Not until you're all better."

"Yeah, you can't move," Casey teased.

She peeled the plastic off two Band-Aids and stuck one on each cheek. "Okay, now I'm going to fix your head wound with this." Emma unrolled a piece of gauze and held it out in front of her. "You have to be very, very, still."

"I won't move a muscle," Ben said.

Emma proceeded to wrap the gauze from his chin, around the side of his face, and over his head and then tied it in a knot. She looked back at Casey who was still sitting on the edge of the bed next to Ben. "Did you check his chest and legs yet?"

With the stethoscope sitting around her neck Casey started to move the flat chest piece over his chest.

"No, Mom. You have to put the things in your ears and do it for real."

Casey lifted the hollow metal tubes and placed the earpieces in her ears. She moved the chest piece over his body as she'd done a thousand times. *All people enjoy the mall,* she thought. It was a mnemonic she learned in medical school about the cardiac auscultation locations: aortic, pulmonic, Erb's point, tricuspid, mitral.

The first sound occurs when the mitral valve and the tricuspid valve close. The second sound occurs when the aortic valve and the pulmonary valve close after the blood leaves your heart. Ultimately a healthy heart has a regular rhythm and makes a lub-dub sound each time it beats. What she heard wasn't a regular rhythm.

Casey moved the chest piece around several more times and then let the stethoscope hang freely while she checked his pulse. Arrhythmia is best determined with an EKG or EPS, but sometimes checking the regularity of a pulse can also help.

She held his wrist firmly for a count of fifteen, but this time she didn't feel any irregularity. Maybe her mind was just playing tricks on her?

"So, am I good to go, Doc?" Ben asked.

Casey looked over at Emma. "What do you think Miss Nurse? Is he all better now?"

"You will need lots of fluid and rest," Emma said. "But you are all better."

Ben held out his hand and Emma shook it. "Thank you so much. I don't know what I would have done without you."

"Alright. Now it's time to get ready for bed. Clean up and I'll come back in here in a bit."

"But, Mom…"

Casey shot Emma a quick look and she acquiesced.

"Okay…"

* * *

After Emma was asleep, Casey started cleaning the kitchen again.

He walked up behind her and wrapped his arms around her waist. She stopped cleaning for a moment, but didn't respond to several soft kisses on her shoulder.

"Is something on your mind?" Ben asked.

Casey turned around to face him, her lower back and hands pressed against the counter while Ben's hands moved up to her shoulders. "Can I ask you a question without you getting offended?"

Ben smiled. "That's not usually the start of a good conversation."

"Do you know what Erythropoietin is?"

"EPO? Yeah, why?"

She swallowed back a small block of fear. "Have you ever taken it?"

"Yeah, I mean, who doesn't blood dope these days?"

Her face went completely flush and she straightened up, pushing him back a little. "Ben, I'm serious. Do you?"

"No, of course I don't do EPO. Why would you even ask that?"

Casey looked down at the sink where a Lima bean was smashed against the sidewall.

"Casey?"

"Your heart," she said.

"What about it?"

"Earlier when we were playing I thought I heard an arrhythmia and it just kind of scared me. But then I checked your pulse and couldn't feel anything, so it was probably nothing."

Two small tears started at the corner of her eyes and ran slowly down the sides of her face.

Ben wiped away each tear with the edge of his thumbs. "Come here," he said, pulling her towards him. He wrapped his arms around her as she buried her face in his chest.

She knew she liked Ben a lot, but she hadn't realized it until this very moment that she loved him. And that's what scared her so much earlier, just the thought of something bad happening. "I'm sorry," she said.

"For what?"

"For crying. I feel like I'm always crying."

Ben ran his fingers over her back, gently scratching through the fabric of her shirt. "You know what they say about tears. It's not a sign of weakness, it's a sign of being strong for too long."

She tucked her arms in between her chest and his and looked up at him. He lowered his head until it rested against hers and their eyes were just inches apart.

She knew there was never a good time to say this in a relationship. She knew that guys took it completely different than girls sometimes. She knew what she was risking. And yet, none of that seemed to matter because more than anything she knew that it was true.

"I love you," she said.

Ben looked back at her and said, "I love you first."

# 42

## Kiss Me

*May 12, 2015*

Two days later Casey sat uncomfortably in a small plastic chair inside the Shands Teaching Hospital wing. One of the residents had put together a lecture on atrial fibrillation based on a recent case. She swung the wooden leaf desktop over her lap and sat her iPad on top of it.

To her left was a full height brick wall, but to her right was a wall of almost entirely all windows that looked out to a small courtyard. Casey stared out the window, distracted, thinking about Ben.

Yesterday was the start of summer classes and the first day in a couple weeks she hadn't seen Ben. His coach had called an impromptu meeting to discuss a change in travel arrangements for the SEC Championship in Tuscaloosa. They talked last night for a little bit, and he promised to stop by sometime today before they left.

She wanted to go so bad, but there was just no way. She couldn't even imagine asking for three days off as a first year, even though she was technically only six weeks away from being a second year resident. Plus there was Emma, and her school.

Several nurses walked outside towards a concrete bench with identical Vera Bradley lunch boxes that looked more like large hand purses. Casey's attention turned back to her lecture as the lights in the lecture hall turned off and a Power Point presentation popped up on the white dry erase boards at the front of the classroom.

A cute Asian girl stood off to the right, while a pudgy white guy started talking. Casey couldn't remember his name, but it was something like William, or Todd. One of those names that made you think he was going to barely finish residency in time to get his trust fund that couldn't be opened until he turned thirty.

*Ugh, stop being such a bitch and just pay attention.*

Several female residents in front of her started chatting, and then another small group to her left as well. *Seriously? I'm finally trying to pay attention…*

A couple of them pointed towards the right side of the room. Casey looked over to her right, thinking maybe someone had walked in late or something, but there was no one there.

The pudgy guy kept on talking, so enthralled in hearing himself speak that he didn't even notice no one was paying attention. Even the cute Asian girl standing next to him was now looking to the right as well.

Casey looked to the right again. *Seriously, what are they…*

That's when she saw him. Ben was in the courtyard outside the lecture hall stretching his hams and quads on the bench seat at the table next to where the nurses were sitting.

Another runner was with him. Casey watched as they both bent down on their right knee and pulled their right foot towards their back. They held it for a few seconds and then switched sides.

From this angle she had a perfect view of his profile. She could see his left quad tighten as he pulled his foot closer and closer to the blue nylon shorts that were also being stretched tight against his muscles.

His stomach flexed and her eyes traced the outline of his obliques up to the lines that formed his chest, and then down to just below his waist where they tucked tightly into his shorts.

She continued to watch as he stood up and walked over to the nurses' table. He was smiling as they talked and then they pointed towards the windows that Casey was sitting behind. She looked around and it seemed like most of the class, even some of the guys, were watching him.

She tried to quietly get up, but forgot about her iPad and almost knocked it off the desk as she stood. Several students looked back at her. "Sorry," she whispered.

She walked quickly up the ramp that led out of the auditorium and opened the door to the courtyard. The sunlight met her smile with instant warmth and Ben turned around as the door shut behind her.

She looked over at the windows to see if anyone was still watching as she walked towards him, but they were tinted and she could only see a small reflection of the courtyard instead.

"I thought you were stopping by later?" Casey said, still unable to wipe the smile from her lips.

"Kiss me," he said.

"What?" she asked, surprised at his choice of words.

He stepped closer. "Kiss me."

His voice was calm and steady, almost commanding. His body language was the same as that one night he snuck into her window, as if he were here for one thing and one thing only.

Her body tingled as the warmth of the sun spread over her, coaxing away the goosebumps from the frigid hospital.

Ben pinched the fabric near the waist of her scrubs and pulled her closer and until she had to put her hands on his bare stomach to stop him. As her fingers felt the firm creases in his stomach, he repeated himself one more time. "Kiss me."

Her body betrayed her mind and she raised up on her toes moving closer to his lips. His warm hands slid softly over her arms, reversing the job the sun had started, and sending chills throughout the rest of her body. She wasn't prepared for the sensation of his lips against hers. With his hands barely touching her it felt as if his lips held her entire body.

Casey opened her eyes and realized everyone in the courtyard was staring straight at them. The nurses at the bench, the attending doctors across the way, the guy that Ben was running with. She could feel all of their eyes.

"I'll try to call or text when I can," Ben said.

Casey nodded.

"And we can hang out Sunday after work, if you don't have other plans?"

"That sounds perfect."

Ben smiled at her and then nodded over at the guy standing behind him. He was about to take off when Casey said, "To give anything less than your best is to sacrifice the gift." It was a famous quote from Steve Prefontaine, the guy Ben was always talking about.

Ben paused for a moment holding her gaze. "As weird as this sounds, that may be the hottest thing you've ever said to me." He leaned in and kissed her one more time and took off running, leaving Casey standing there smiling.

When she walked back in, she tried to keep her head down, using the same elementary philosophy that if you never make eye contact with your teacher, they can't call on you. But this wasn't elementary school. Several of the male residents stood up and started making that horribly annoying hooting thing that guys do. "Whoo whoo woo!"

Casey was so unbelievably embarrassed and then the girls joined in with their higher pitched cheers. Even pudgy Tom had stopped talking and was now clapping. Casey didn't know what to do so she just stood there blushing, with her hand over her lips where Ben's had just been.

\* \* \*

"Man, was that your girl?" Brad said as he and Ben jogged alongside Center Road, back towards campus. Parker bailed on their run today, so Brad had tagged along. "That body. That face. Man, I'd…"

Ben interrupted him. "Are you familiar with the phrase 'when all you have is a hammer?'"

Brad looked at Ben kind of confused as they ran. "No, why?"

"Because I'm going to give you the benefit of the doubt and assume your previous words were going to be something along the lines of, 'Man I'd like to be friends with her, because she looks like such a nice girl.' Because if I happened to believe you were thinking disrespectful thoughts about that girl back there, well…then you're going to find out why every problem I have is a nail."

Brad didn't say another word the rest of the workout.

# 43

## REGIONALS

*May 16, 2015*

Ben sat alone in a crimson padded fold out chair in the University of Alabama locker rooms. It felt like he had been doing nothing but sitting since they arrived in Tuscaloosa four days ago.

He looked up at the black and white clock on the wall. It was 5:23 p.m. on Saturday afternoon and the only event that remained was the Men's 5000 meter. To most people at the University of Florida the race didn't mean a single thing because Florida had already secured enough points to win the Southeastern Conference Championships and a trip to next month's NCAA Championships. For most people this was a race for second between Texas A&M and Arkansas. Not to Ben.203

Ben leaned forward resting his elbows on his knees as he rolled his wrists in small circles. He opened and closed his hands flexing muscles all the way up to his shoulder. He felt tight.

He closed his eyes and tried to think of something, anything. But all he could see was the inexplicable darkness. He recalled the last words Casey said to him before he left. *To give anything less than your best is to sacrifice the gift.*

The door to the locker room opened and Ben could hear the cacophony of noises from the crowd.

Parker stepped into the doorway, the sun behind him creating a silhouette. "It's time," he said.

The words reverberated through him like the echo of the crowd against the stands. *It's time.*

# 44

## CHARTS AND RECORDS

*May 16, 2015*

Casey had been sitting in the resident's workroom for the past hour, charting and scheduling out-patient consultations. All the other interns, except one, had already gone home for the day, and it was her turn to wait to hand off the team's patients to the night intern.

Melissa sat across from her, re-reviewing patient charts. Ever heard of a paranoid patient? Well, Melissa was a paranoid doctor. A good doctor, but paranoid nonetheless. She put down her charts and looked up at Casey. "You need any help updating the patient list?"

That was another thing about Melissa. She always wanted to help. Which can be good, or bad, depending on how you look at it. "I'm good," Casey said. "Almost done anyways."

Melissa walked over to the television hanging from one of those corner wall mounts and flipped it on. "Hey, Casey," she said.

Casey ignored her for the moment, she was almost done and her co-intern would be here shortly so she could leave.

"Casey," Melissa said again, and again Casey ignored her.

"Isn't that your boy on T.V.?"

Casey looked up. After the whole thing in the courtyard a few days ago, everyone finally knew she was dating Benson Wilder, University of Florida track star. And kisser extraordinaire. The girls would tease her and then tell her how jealous they were, while the guys resorted to giving her hi-fives, whatever that meant. So, for a moment she thought Melissa was just teasing her.

Then she looked up and saw Melissa staring at a group of runners rounding an orange track. Casey was too far away from the T.V. to see anything, so she stood up and walked closer until she was standing right next to Melissa, looking up at the screen. "I thought he said they weren't airing the regionals," she said more to herself than to Melissa.

Melissa answered anyways though. "I don't think they are. They just cut to this and the announcer said something about some record."

Casey looked at the screen. In the bottom right was Ben's current time, followed by his projected time, followed by the SEC record. The record was 13:41, and he was projected to run a 13:22. He was nineteen seconds fast. She thought back to what he told her on their first date. *A single second is a lifetime on the track.*

He wasn't just going to break the record, he was going to shatter it.

The cameraman zoomed out and showed the considerable lead Ben had on the rest of the group.

"He's really fast," Melissa said.

There were so many different records it was hard to say what any of them even meant. Yet, having already won the race, Ben pushed himself harder. Cemoy Kampbell from Arkansas had hung with Ben for most of it, but now even he fell forty to fifty feet back.

The fans in the crowd cheered and the announcer went wild. His teammates began to scream and yell. They all thought one thing, and one thing only: Ben wasn't just trying to win, he was trying to break the SEC meet record.

The only person who thought differently was standing a thousand miles away in small hospital room. She knew he was trying to hold on to some distant piece of himself that he believed he could only find when he was running on edge. She knew that the records were just numbers without meaning. And it scared her to think how hard he was pushing himself right now.

Ben crossed the finish line and the camera panned back to the others as they came in behind him, and then the channel flipped back to an ESPN broadcaster. "Well, there you have it folks. Benson Wilder of the University of Florida has just broken a twelve-year-old SEC meet record with a time of 13:21:54. More on that later, but for now back to the Braves and Marlins, where Atlanta still leads 5-3."

# 45

## ONCE IN A LIFETIME

*May 17, 2015*

Even though it was Sunday the stadium was packed when the white motor coach turned in. Attached to the front of the huge bus was a white banner that read "Here Come The Gators." Casey was standing alongside Nikki, and thousands of other friends and family. She had dropped Emma off at a friend's house just before lunch.

As the bus drove onto the track "I Gotta Feeling" by Black Eyed Peas started playing over the loudspeakers. The crowd was starting to pick up with energy holding up signs, clapping, whistling, yelling. Really anything they could do to make noise.

The bus pulled to a stop on the track in front of the bleachers and the front folding doors swung open. A security guard stepped off first followed by the coaching staff.

Different sections in the crowd cheered louder as their friend stepped off the bus. Casey recognized a lot of the guys, but didn't know some of their names. She saw the guy that visited her at the hospital with Ben the day before she left. And then she saw Parker. He had a huge smile on his face as he stepped off holding his finger emphatically toward the crowd as he yelled "Number one!"

The last person off the bus was Ben. He waved to the crowd with a smile as an electric current of cheers lit up the stadium. Casey and Nikki cheered along with them.

The music coming from the loudspeakers died down as someone began to speak. "Ladies and gentlemen. Please welcome the Outdoor Track and Field 2015 Southeastern Conference Champions. Yourrrrrr Florrrrriiiidddaaaa Gators!"

Again the grandstand of over 5,000 people erupted.

Coach Melvick walked up to the microphone and said a few words, congratulating the team and thanking the fans and families for their support.

Casey looked back at Ben and his eyes were locked on hers. It wasn't a serious gaze, but playful. He was smiling. He looked genuinely happy.

The seats emptied when Coach Melvick finished talking and everyone scattered amongst the team congratulating them in person. Nikki and Casey stood near the fence trying to separate from the crowd, but they didn't see Ben.

"You're Casey, right?"

Casey turned her attention to the left where one of the runners was standing. She recognized him, but didn't know his name. "Umm, yes…"

"Okay Ben said he'd meet you over there." He pointed to his right towards the athletic center.

"And why are *you* telling me this?" Casey said.

"He told me to find you."

Casey looked over and Nikki and she just shrugged. "Okay, thanks."

The kid jogged off and Casey and Nikki headed towards the large brick building at the south end of the bleachers. Though as they approached they didn't see Ben.

"You ladies wouldn't happen to be looking for me, would you?"

Casey turned around to find Ben leaning against the wall that run along the side of the concrete grandstand.

Ben pushed off the wall and took several steps towards Casey. He bent down and pressed his lips to hers, lifting the bottom of her chin gently with his right hand.

"No problem," Nikki said. "You two make out. I'll just stand over here and watch. It's not awkward or anything."

Casey pulled away from Ben and looked over at Nikki. "Sorry," she said with a smile.

"I think Parker was looking for you," Ben said.

Nikki pointed to herself. "Me?"

"Yo Ben!" Parker yelled running up to them. "Ben," he said again looking around. "Casey. Nikki." He stopped talking when he looked at Nikki.

Ben snapped his fingers. "Hello?"

"What?" Parker said.

"You just came running over here yelling my name."

"Oh, ya. They want you to come hold up the trophy for some pictures."

Ben sighed.

"It's such a rough life you have," Casey joked.

"I hate this stuff. I'll be back in like five minutes."

"Okay," Casey said. "I'll probably just hang out over here."

"Get a drink," Parker blurted out.

"He means, do you want to get a drink," Ben said. "They got a table of Gatorade and pizza and stuff over there."

Casey smiled as she watched the interaction between Parker and Nikki.

"Are you going to run away from me this time?" Nikki said.

Parker blushed. "That was totally out of my control."

Nikki looked back at Casey. "I'm fine right here."

"I'll bring you back something," Nikki said.

Casey watched as Parker and Nikki followed Ben between the crowds of people near the bus. Even in the daylight the cameras flashed brightly. Several reporters held their smartphones out like tape recorders and began asking Ben questions again.

She walked up several steps to the first row in the bleachers and sat down. She saw Coach Melvick excuse himself from several people and head away from the crowds. He must not like this stuff either, Casey thought. She was surprised when he turned to walk up the steps towards her instead of heading straight towards the double doors of the athletic center that led to his office.

Coach Melvick sat down a few feet away from her and leaned back so his shoulders were resting on the seat behind him. He let out a sigh as he looked up towards the clouds. Did he know who she was, Casey thought. Was he going to warn her that Ben didn't need any distractions before the NCAA Championships in a few weeks? *Do I introduce myself?*

"You know much about flowers?" Coach Melvick said randomly.

"Flowers?" Casey said confused.

"Me either," he said. "But, my wife loves 'em. She must have a hundred different types at home. I couldn't even tell you the name of one, but she's got them all memorized. Latin names and all."

"That's impressive," Casey said, not really sure why he was telling her this.

Coach Melvick ran his hand over the gray stubble on his face. "One time she was telling me about this flower that grows somewhere in the mountains. Starts with an 'A' I think."

"Andes?" Casey said.

Coach Melvick snapped his fingers. "That's the one. Apparently there is a plant that will grow for a hundred years or more and only bloom once in a life time."

Casey really had no clue why he was telling her this. Was he talking about Ben? Was he trying to tell her something without actually saying it? When he didn't say anything else she said, "I'm not sure I understand."

For the first time since he sat down he looked over at her. "I think you do Miss Taylor."

*Okay, so he does know who I am.* "Are you talking about Ben?" she asked.

Coach Melvick stood up and started walking down the same steps he came up a few minutes ago. He looked back at her one more time. "Some things only happen once in a lifetime," he said.

Ben came jogging towards her a few minutes later. "Was that Coach?" he asked.

Casey nodded yes.

"What did he want?"

She smiled. "Just something about flowers."

210

# 46

## SUGAR

*May 18, 2015*

Ben was tired, but he was excited when he woke up on Monday morning. It was Casey's day off and Coach had given the team the week off, minus a team meeting this afternoon, since they had another month until the NCAA Championships.

Emma's school started at seven forty-five which meant if he got to Casey's around eight, they could spend the whole day just relaxing.

When he arrived the garage was shut, so he walked up to the front door. Before he could knock, though, the door swung open and Casey jumped on him, wrapping her arms around his neck and her legs around his waist.

"My hero," she said in a terrible southern accent. Then she started giving him little pecks all over his head and face.

He walked inside with her still wrapped around him and kicked the door shut. Laughing, he said, "Who is this strange girl, and what did you do with Casey?"

211

She continued on in the southern accent. "You won the race for your beloved and claimed victory."

Ben sat her on the backside of the couch and looked down at her. "What on earth has gotten into you?"

"You, Sir Runner. Now, take me, take me now." Casey puckered up her lips playfully and Ben laughed.

Ben leaned in to give her a quick kiss, thinking she might taste or smell like alcohol, because right now that was the only explanation he could come up with. She tasted like…cookies.

He looked around the room and to his right, sitting on the kitchen counter, he found his answer. He let go of Casey and she fell backwards onto the couch.

"Hey!" she said as she hit the couch cushion.

Ben walked over to the kitchen and picked up a small tub of Cookies 'n Cream ice cream and a bag of Fudge Filled Chewy Chips Ahoy. He held up both and looked over at Casey who was half-hiding, half-peering over the top of the couch. "Please tell me you are not eating cookies and ice cream at eight o'clock in the morning."

Casey jumped over the couch and came running at Ben, a ball of sugar filled energy. She wrapped her arms around his waist, her legs around the back of his calves, and inched her way up his body. When she reached the top she bombarded his neck with kisses. "My hero," she said. She stopped for a moment and looked at him with the most devious, sensual grin. She leaned in closer until there was almost no space between her lips and his. Then like a cheetah springing on a gazelle, she grabbed the ice cream with her left hand and the cookies with her right, hit the ground and took cover on the couch.

"You have serious problems," Ben said.

Casey pulled out a cookie and dipped it in the ice cream and held it up for him to see. Then she started humming and dancing the cookie around like she was taunting him.

Ben took two steps, dove across the couch, snatched the cookie from her hand and shoved it in his mouth before she could move. She looked at him wide eyed and in complete silence and then jumped on him. They wrestled and tickled each other like five-year-olds, stopping every now and then for a quick cookie break.

This went on for about thirty more minutes and then she crashed on the floor next to him. Her head lay across his chest as he played with her hair until eventually he crashed too.

# 47

## Wingman

*May 26, 2015*

"I can't believe Coach actually gave us a week off practice, only three weeks before the championship," Ben said.

"I can't believe you're taking summer classes," Parker said as he jogged next to Ben.

Ben shrugged with his hands as they continued up Fraternity Row. "It's just two classes. Keeps me busy while Casey is working."

"Dude, I could keep you busy!"

"I'm not judging, but I'm just not into that," Ben joked.

"You ditch me over break, and now you ditch me for the summer."

They were only a few minutes into their run, but the summer heat was already beating down on them. It was still a few days before June and it was already ninety-something degrees out.

Ben and Parker were jogging through their usual route, but campus was crowded again now that summer classes had been in full swing for a couple weeks. They stayed on the road as they passed the stadium, most of the students sticking to the sidewalk.

"I didn't ditch you. I told you, if you need a wing man, I'm here. Besides I thought you were dating some new girl, Becca or something."

"Yeeaahhh, she turned out to be a tad on the crazy side."

"Have you ever noticed how all the girls you date are crazy?"

Parker completely ignored him. "Dude, ten o'clock, orange shorts."

Ben looked slightly to his left and didn't see anything. Then he looked to the right. "Do you not know how a clock works?"

"My ten o'clock," Parker corrected.

Ben didn't even bother arguing with that statement. Instead he followed Parker's field of vision to an unbelievably familiar and unbelievably attractive blonde with her left leg propped up on a brick planter, tying her shoe.

"So far out of your league it's not even funny," Ben said. It wasn't just because the girl was drop dead gorgeous, because she was. It was because that was Sandy Mixon, one of the starting forwards for the girls' soccer team.

"Let's do 'The Jerk' then," Parker said. It was a pick up routine where the wingman, Ben in this instance, acts like a jerk to a girl and the friend, Parker, swoops in to save the day.

"I told you I'm not doing that one ever again. It's just not cool."

"Okay, then how about 'My Sister's Birthday?'" Another pick up routine where they ask the girl for ideas of what to buy their little sister for her birthday. The wingman suggests something off the wall, and the friend suggests something sweet.

"How about you stop with the dumb ideas. Just go stand over there by that bike rack, and I'll handle the rest."

Parker looked at Ben and pointed. "Don't mess this up. She could be the one."

"Just go stand over there."

"I'm just…"

"Go."

"Okay, okay. I'm going."

Parker walked over and leaned against the bike rack, while Ben walked up to Sandy.

"Those are some fancy running shoes for a girl who only plays soccer," Ben said.

Sandy turned around and smiled when she saw Ben. "Hey, Ben," she said. They'd met several times before at the training facility. She happened to sneak in late workouts like he did sometimes. "Congrats on the win, by the way."

"Thanks," he said.

Her eyes scanned over his shirtless body. "You got the NCAAs coming up soon, don't you?"

"In a couple weeks, yeah."

Another girl walked up behind Sandy who looked familiar, but Ben couldn't place the name. "You ready?" she asked. "Oh, hey, Ben."

*Hey, girl who I totally do not know the name of.* "Hey," he said.

"Yeah, I'm ready when you are," Sandy said. She turned to Ben, "I'll catch you around this summer?"

"Yes, but…can you do me a quick favor." He looked over to where Parker was standing. "To your right there is a guy standing by the bike rack, wearing the same blue shorts I have on."

They both looked over at Parker and back to Ben.

"What are the chances I could give him your number?"

Sandy looked at her friend and then back to Ben. "Sure," she said. "He's kinda cute."

"Really?" Ben said, a little astonished.

"Well, he's not some weirdo, is he?"

"No, no. He's my roommate. He's actually on the team as well."

"Okay, then yeah."

A couple minutes later Ben walked over to Parker and handed him a napkin with numbers on it.

Parker looked down at the napkin. "I can't believe that actually worked. But seriously, check out this girl lying in the grass over there."

Ben shook his head and took off jogging in the opposite direction. "Sometimes I don't know why I even bother."

\* \* \*

Five miles later and Ben and Parker were passing by Lake Alice, just about a mile away from their dorms.

"Dude, why are we running like it's regionals all over again," Parker said out of breath.

"We took a week off, man, gotta get back at it." Ben picked up the pace even more. "Now let's go." Ben cut across the road and onto an open grass field at the corner of Museum and Fraternity Row. His legs felt good, even in this summer heat, but something didn't feel right.

His chest felt tight and it was suddenly hard to get a full breath. Sometimes runners breathed erratically when they lost focus, so he tried to calm down and concentrate on his diaphragm, but it didn't help.

Parker passed him on the left. "Let's go, old man," he joked.

Ben didn't even hear him, though. He pushed his right hand over the pain in his chest, but that didn't stop his head from spinning. He tripped over his own feet and hit the ground.

# 48

## Promises

*June 7, 2015*

Casey sat outside in the courtyard, eating lunch with Melissa. She was glad there was no lecture today as she took a bite of leftover alfredo pasta from Olive Garden that Ben had surprised her with last night. Everything had been great for the past couple weeks, since he won regionals. But with the national championships just a couple days away Ben had been more on edge than ever.

She looked up at Melissa, who was inspecting each little carrot stick before she dipped it in ranch dressing and took a bite. "Do you think anything will really change when we officially become second-years?"

Melissa looked down at her next carrot and then up at Casey. "I think July is going to suck, then it might get a little better."

"Why do you say that?"

"Apparently all the attendings take vacation so they don't have to deal with orientation of the new interns, which just gets pushed farther and farther down the line until eventually we get to babysit them."

That actually didn't sound bad at all to Casey. A lot of the attendings were kind of a-holes anyways. She finished the last bite of her pasta and pulled out the last breadstick. It was still warm when she picked it up, the garlic-butter spread glistening in the sun. "I love you, Mr. Breadstick," she said just before she took a huge bite.

Melissa looked over as Casey chewed and she couldn't tell if she was jealous because she was stuck with carrots and celery, or repulsed by how much food Casey had just shoved in her mouth. The fact that she was talking to her food probably didn't help her cause any.

Casey was about to finish off the breadstick in one more huge bite when a familiar face walked out of the hospital and into the courtyard.

"Parker?" Casey said.

He looked over at the sound of his name, and she looked around for Ben.

"Hey," Parker said as he walked up to her table. "Can we talk?"

She was a little caught off guard at his question. He looked serious, but she couldn't help but think it there was probably a girl at the hospital he wanted her introduce him to. "Uh, yeah." She looked around for a place to talk. "We can go…"

"You can sit here," Melissa said getting up from the table. She snapped the lid back on her plastic container. "I think there's a fly in my ranch now anyways."

Parker sat down across from Casey after Melissa left.

"What's up?" Casey said.

Parker looked down, averting eye contact.

"Parker?"

Parker looked up at Casey and she could tell something was definitely wrong. Not like how-to-ask-a-girl-out wrong, but like wrong-wrong. He started to get up. "I'm sorry. I shouldn't have bothered you at work."

"Parker," Casey said again. "What's going on?"

Parker hesitated for a minute and then sat back down. "He made me promise not to tell anyone, but I think something is wrong."

"Who made you promise? Ben?"

Parker nodded his head, and Casey tried to keep calm. Emergency medicine 101: ensure the patient is safe from any immediate danger. "Where is Ben right now?"

Parker looked down at his Apple Watch. "I'm supposed to meet him at Gator Dining in about ten minutes."

He didn't actually answer the question, but at least she knew he was okay.

"Okay, now what do you think is wrong?"

Parker just shook his head and stood up from the table. She could tell this time he wasn't going to sit back down. "I promised Ben I wouldn't say anything, but I think you should just talk to him."

Casey stood up and walked several steps in front of Parker, blocking his exit. "Parker. What is going on?"

"I'm sorry," he said. "I shouldn't have even said as much as I did. Just talk to him, please."

Casey watched Parker walk away and she felt as scared as the day she found out Emma might never see again.

# 49

## GRACE

*June 7, 2015*

A couple hours later Parker walked down the hall a few steps ahead of Ben returning from Gator Dining singing the same stupid song he had been singing all day: "*But I would walk five hundred miles, and I would walk five hundred more. To be the man who walked five thousand miles…*"

"For the love of all creatures that can hear. Geez, those aren't even the right words," Ben said.

Parker turned around. "How are those not the right words?"

"Think about it, if you walk five hundred miles, and then five hundred more, how is that five thousand?"

For a moment Parker seemed completely lost, and then it clicked and he kept on walking. He turned the corner where four chairs sat around a small circular table just outside their dorm room and continued singing. "To be the man who walked one thousand miles—"

Parker stopped abruptly—the moment he saw Casey. It wasn't that he was embarrassed or trying to avoid being obnoxious around her. It was the mixed emotions spread across her body as she stood their leaning against the door. It was something between terribly sad and terribly angry. Either way he knew, he didn't want to stick around long enough to find out which one. Because he also knew he might be the cause.

"Finally," Ben said, noticing the peace and quiet. Parker nearly knocked Ben over as they both rounded the corner going in opposite directions.

"What the…where are you going?" Ben said to Parker, who was walking unusually fast *away* from their room.

"I forgot something," Parker said over his shoulder.

"What did you forget?"

Parker didn't answer. He just pushed open the glass panel door and kept walking.

"Okay…" Ben said to himself. Walking into the community room, he reached into his pocket to grab his keys. Across the room he saw Casey standing arms crossed, and understood exactly where Parker was going.

\* \* \*

Asking a girl what's wrong can sometimes be like asking a starving lion in the middle of a jungle if he'd like to eat you. Instead Ben opted for a hug and kiss, neither of which went exceedingly well.

Ben unlocked the door and Casey walked in. He followed behind her and for a moment considered the fact that if he closed it, no one would be able to hear him scream…

Casey walked over and sat on the edge of the bed, sitting her purse down next to her.

Ben looked at the clock by his bed. It was one of those retro steel framed alarm clocks with the twin bells on top. The kind that made that ticking noise every time the second hand moved. The kind that drove Parker crazy. It was 6:41 p.m.

"I thought I was coming to your place tonight?"

Casey didn't respond at first, instead she just watched him. And then she said an all too familiar line. "Is there something you want to tell me?"

Ben thought about the question for a moment, knowing there was only one possible explanation: Parker told her what happened.

Ben turned away from her and sat down on the end of the bed. "I'm assuming Parker talked to you today?"

Casey nodded.

"What did he say?"

"He just said that something was wrong and I needed to talk to you."

"He didn't say about what?"

"No, he wouldn't say."

Ben looked down at the comforter and began picking at one of the clear threads.

She didn't understand why he wouldn't want to reveal whatever he was hiding. What could possibly be harder to tell her than what he already had?

"I've been having some problems running," he finally said.

"What kind of problems?"

"Sometimes I can't breathe and my chest tightens up."

Trying to stay calm, Casey thought back to the arrhythmia that she had dismissed a few weeks ago. "Okay, what did the trainers say?"

"I don't know," he said, looking back down at the comforter.

"You don't know?" Casey asked, confused.

"I mean, I haven't told them."

This conversation was starting to make absolutely zero sense. Nothing was adding up. It all just seemed like a series of random facts. She kept on trying to work it out in her head.

*Obviously Parker must have seen something happen to Ben when he was running…so he came to tell her because Ben was refusing to tell anyone. What is the one thing Ben wouldn't want to talk about? His daughter…* "Ben," she said.

He looked up at her.

She didn't want to ask this question. She hated the way it sounded as she said it to herself, but he wasn't giving her any choice. "How exactly did your daughter die?" She knew the answer was medical complications, and she had left it at that when he told her, but now she needed details.

Ben stood up from the bed and walked towards the door. For a minute Casey thought he might be done with the conversation. That she had asked a question he couldn't quite handle yet.

"She had hypertrophy cardiomyopathy," he said over his shoulder. "She died during a heart transplant."

"Is it congenital?"

"I don't know."

"How do you not know?" Casey said, almost angry. "What did the test results reveal?"

"I never got tested."

"Okay," Casey said, fishing around in her mind for options. "That's not a big deal. I know some of the cardiologists at Shands. I can talk to them tomorrow and—"

"I'm not getting tested."

"Ben."

He turned around and the look in his eyes had changed. He didn't seem distant anymore. He didn't seem lost in a sea of memories. He seemed lucid. He seemed determined.

"Ben," she said again, softly getting up from the bed. "You know you can't keep running if you have this condition, right?"

Ben moved back towards the door. "Do you want to go for a walk?" he said, completely avoiding the question.

"A walk? What? No, I don't want to go for a walk. I want you to tell me you're not still planning on running this weekend."

Ben opened the door. "I'm just going to get some fresh air real quick."

Casey grabbed her purse and ran after him. "Ben," she said.

He kept walking until he pushed open the heavy aluminum door that led outside.

"Ben!" Casey yelled again.

Ben looked up through the dusky sky towards the faint yellow glow of the moon.

Casey walked up next to him. "Ben, if you have this condition…"

"*If* I have the condition," he interrupted her.

"Okay, so let's go get you tested."

"I leave tomorrow for the NCAA Championship." Ben took a step off the curb and onto Fraternity Row. A car came speeding by and honked several times.

Casey walked along the grass next to him. "Ben, why are you doing this? I don't understand."

Ben stopped and looked at her. "I'm not asking you to understand."

"You let me think everything was okay that night I listened to your heart and was so concerned."

"It is okay."

"No!" she yelled. "It's not okay."

He started to walk away again, but she stepped in front of him. "I understand you love to run. Trust me, I do. But what is so important about running that you're willing to die for it?"

He didn't respond. He didn't even move.

"Ben, please, you can't run until you at least get tested to make sure everything is okay."

"I can't," he said.

"What? You can't what?"

"I can't give up."

"Ben this is not giving up."

"That's exactly what it is!" he yelled.

Casey looked back at him. He had never yelled at her before, and it scared her, but losing him scared her even more. And that's why she said, "What about Grace?"

Ben's eyes burned into hers at the sound of his daughter's name and he stepped closer to Casey. His voice was calm now as he spoke. "When Grace was in the hospital, she always asked me to tell her stories. But the problem was I didn't know a lot of kid stories. I spent all my days in some cruddy orphanage just hoping I could make it through the night. So, I

227

would tell her about me running in high school and all the different competitions. She always wanted to know how she could be a runner just like her dad, and I always told her great runners only have one thing in common: They never give up."

"You have to know this isn't the same thing. You could die."

"I'm sorry, Casey. I can't quit."

There was only one more thing Casey could say to convince him, and she wasn't even sure if she meant it. "If you leave tomorrow and put your life on the line for some stupid race, then…I can't promise I'll be here for you when you get back."

Ben didn't even hesitate before he walked away from her. "I'm not asking you to."

# 50

## FORGET ME NOT

*June 8, 2015*

The next morning, an hour before the bus took off for the airport there was nothing but silence surrounding Ben as he stood upon the sacred ground. The wind lifted itself around him and danced between the leaves and branches above, but even the trees fell silent today.

Ben knelt down and pressed his hand against the weathered granite. The damp morning grass soaked into his pants. He could feel the windblown fragments lightly scrape against his skin as he ran his fingers over her name: Grace Lynn Wilder.

He tried to abandon his own mind, to leave it behind in this place where only souls can speak. And for a moment he did, until he reached into his front shirt pocket and pulled out a flower with five petals and a golden center.

He twirled it around in his hand several times and laid it atop her grave. No one knew where the tradition of placing flowers at gravesites came from, or why people did it. Most people didn't even understand the significance of a particular flower. But Ben did.

This flower was called forget-me-not and it signified the only thing he had left of his daughter: memories.

The wind died down long enough for the flower to rest there peacefully. He turned his eyes towards the headstone to the right, and moved up alongside it. Two words stood out above the rest: mother and wife. He stared at them with an empty mind and a full heart, until the world let him know it was time to leave with a swift breeze that lifted the flower into the air.

For several seconds, though, Ben didn't move. Instead he whispered several words.

"Lord, I do not know how you want us to pray for those who are no longer with us. I simply ask that you know the fullness of my heart and let that be enough."

All of time seemed to sit still, until Ben finally stood.

# 51

## EVERYTHING

*June 12, 2015*

They had arrived in Eugene on Monday, two days before the event started. Coach wanted them to have a couple days to get acclimated to the Pacific Northwest.

On Wednesday the hurdles, relays, hammer throw, javelin throw, and shot put were completed. On Thursday it was the pole vault, long jump, and steeplechase. That just left the high jump, triple jump, sprints, and long distance for Friday.

Ben woke before the sun. He looked down at his phone, but he had no messages. He hadn't spoken to Casey in almost four days, which was the longest he'd gone without speaking to her since he first saw her that day on campus. He scrolled through his contacts until his thumb hovered over the picture next to her name. For a moment he thought about calling her, just to tell her how much he loved her, how much he missed her. Even if she answered though, he knew what she'd say. So, instead he set it back on the nightstand by his bed.

He got ready as quietly as he could and made his way to the stadium in the dark.

The streets in Eugene, Oregon, were empty and cold, except for the man curled up next to a yellow lab underneath a small Aspen. The dog looked up as he passed, but the man didn't move beneath his dark green jacket.

The track was only a few blocks away, and technically he wasn't supposed to go anywhere without one of the coaches or student managers, but he didn't think it was necessary to wake anyone for his race day ritual.

The grounds crew was already busy working by the time he arrived. The lights above the stands would be turning off soon, but for now they buzzed brightly with dirty yellow light.

Ben sat his bag down in the grass and tossed his blue and white flip-flops down next to it. He walked a single lap around the inside lane of the track, letting his bare feet feel every subtle rise and fall. Every loose piece of rubber. Every slick or coarse section revealing itself.

Today was day three of the 2015 NCAA Championships, and the 5000 meter was the last race of the event. The track would run slightly different in the afternoon as it would at dawn, and Ben wished he didn't have to wait all day.

He slipped his flip-flops back on and walked up the stadium stairs until he was a few rows up and looked out at the track.

A voice from behind startled him. "You know I saw this kid run in high school once."

Ben turned around to find Coach Melvick sitting several rows farther up.

"Coach?" Ben said.

"I never paid too much attention to a lot of the runners in Florida. I never much thought they even knew why people ran. But…" he said as he clasped his hands together. "There was this one runner that everyone kept talking about. He wasn't tall and lean like him, but everyone said this kid had the greatest kick since Lasse Virén."

Ben listened as Coach kept talking.

"You know I was freshman at Oregon in '72 when Virén beat Prefontaine. You know some people cried when Pre lost? It was that damn beautiful of a race. So…about six years ago when I heard about this kid from Ocala, Florida, with a kick like Virén, I had to check it out.

"A lot of the coaches waited to take the trek down there during the State Championships. But I wanted to see what the kid would do on just any other race day. So, I drove down one day when they were racing some shit schools in some shit meet. It was an absolutely miserable Florida day. Not a cloud in the sky, damn sun beating down on my neck so hard I thought my head might literally roll off my shoulders."

Coach laughed to himself. "Fucking miserable."

"Anyways, the race gets going, and it was the 10,000 meter if I recall. And I'm watching this seventeen-year-old kid that's about five feet, ten inches, 185 pounds. Looked more like a baseball player than a runner." He grunted out another laugh.

"Twenty-six minutes or so pass and I see the lead group of runners in the distance. The damn kid was running out there to the side of them like he was lost or something. Then out of nowhere the kid just takes off. I mean takes off. It was too early, though. There was about 500 meters left, and I knew at about the 150 meter mark he was just gonna die."

Coach let out a deep breath into the morning air.

"But he didn't. That little shit just kept running faster, and faster, and faster. I headed home that afternoon and over the next few weeks I'd get calls every now and then from some of the other coaches asking me if I thought he was the real deal. Did he really have a better kick than Virén?"

Coach locked eyes on Ben. "You know what I told them?"

Ben shook his head no.

"I told them he couldn't out-kick Virén if Virén was running backwards."

"You know I broke every 5,000 meter and 10,000 meter high school record in the nation, right?" Ben said.

"Yeah, I know you did, kid."

Coach stood up and walked slowly down the steps. "You just never figured out how you did it."

"We'll see this afternoon when I break the collegiate record," Ben said.

Coach laughed again. "Break the record? Not if you hang back and try to out-kick Kevin Robinson, you won't."

"That's how I run. That's how I've always ran."

"I know, kid. And maybe it's my fault for letting you. But, if you run like that today, you'll be licking the dust off Mr. Robinson's shoes by the time you reach the finish line."

"This is impeccable fucking timing you have. What the hell am I supposed to do now?"

"You don't want to really know, kid."

Ben reached his hand out towards Coach Melvick's shoulders, stopping him as he took several steps down the stands. "Coach. I want to know."

Coach Melvick hesitated as he looked at Ben. Then he let out a deep breath. "Alright," he said. "If you want to win today then it's quite simple. You hang back and draft off Robinson for about the first four thousand meters."

"And then?" Ben asked.

"Well, then you sprint to the finish."

Ben laughed. "Coach that's like the last two laps of the race. No one can sprint that."

Coach continued walking down the bleacher stairs and looked back up at Ben one more time. "No one could do anything until they did it, kid."

# 52

## WORDS

*June 12, 2015*

It was just past one in the afternoon when Casey got home. She had hit the eighty-hour mark that morning and was sent home after spending most of the previous night in the hospital, some idiots at a bar not realizing that hitting each other with broken beer bottles wasn't a good idea. Luckily no one was killed, but one of the guys needed over forty stitches from the bottom of his jaw to just below his eye. It was the most sutures she had ever given a single person.

After she set her stuff down on the kitchen table, she was surprised she even had enough energy to make it all the way to her bed. There were no words to describe how good her down comforter pillow felt beneath her.

The feeling lasted all of ten seconds before she heard the high-pitch chime of her doorbell.

"Go away," she said. Face down into her pillow it sounded more like *gho uhwuuhh*.

The person at the door apparently decided that knocking was the next logical step.

Casey reluctantly sat up and went to answer it. Opening the door, she found a full-faced, red-haired women dressed in navy slacks and a light blue polo. She held an envelope in her left hand and a dark gray handheld wireless gadget in her right.

"Good afternoon!" the lady said in an unbelievably cheerful voice. She looked down at the name on the envelope. "Miss Taylor?"

"Yes," Casey said, also nodding her head.

The woman handed her the letter and said, "I just need you to sign here and we're good to go."

Casey initialed her name quickly and handed the device back to the woman.

"Last name, please?" the woman said.

"Umm, Taylor," Casey said. "You just asked me that."

"Sorry, ma'am, have to follow protocol. Have a good day!"

"You…too…" Casey said as she closed the door.

She looked down at the letter. In the top left corner it said, "RestoreSight.org," followed by a blue and green half-moon that Casey guessed was supposed to be an eye. The name sounded familiar but she couldn't place it, probably because she felt like she could fall asleep just standing there if she had to. She sat the letter on the dining room table and then walked back towards the silk duvet, down comforter, and full body pillows calling her name.

She hit the mattress for the second time and she suddenly recognized the name "Restore Sight." That was the donor organization that had found a corneal transplant for Emma about a year ago.

She got back up and retrieved the letter. She slid her finger under the crease and ripped the envelope cleanly along its spine. She found a letter folded in thirds along with another envelope, though this one contained no addresses or names on the outside.

*Dear Miss Taylor,*

*June 9, 2015 marks the one-year anniversary of Emma Taylor's corneal transplantation. We wish her the best and hope she is living a very colorful life.*

*Our files indicate that you elected to be notified if the donor chooses to be identified after the required twelve-month anonymous period.*

*Please note that you are not obligated to read or reply to this letter, and this is a courtesy letter based on your decision to be notified twelve months prior. You may contact us at 1-800-437-3937 for any additional inquiries.*

*Enclosed you will find a sealed envelope with the information you have requested, along with any notes the donor or donor's guardian have requested to be passed on.*

*Sincerely,*

*The Restore Sight Team*

# 53

## HITTING THE WALL

*June 12, 2005*

Ben still hung back in the middle group, just one to two strides behind Kevin Robinson.

The runners continued to bump and elbow for position even as they crossed the starting area to complete their ninth lap.

All the coaches yelled to their runners as they passed, but Coach Melvick just did the same thing he'd done for the last nine laps: He simply nodded his head.

Ben still didn't know if what Coach wanted him to do was possible. But as he took the first turn of lap ten, it didn't really matter. He could feel the lactic acid building up inside his muscles. It felt like his muscles were balloons and someone was blowing more air into them than they could hold.

His concentration broke and instead of nothingness he could hear everything. His bib flapping repeatedly against his jersey. The perpetual pounding of his shoes against the track. The breath of all the runners around him heavy and forced.

Two runners pushed passed him and he was suddenly more than five strides behind Robinson. He had hit the wall: a feeling of false fatigue that every runner feared.

In about forty seconds, the lead group would be starting lap eleven. At that point sprinting the last two laps would be the least of his concerns. Because if Ben didn't break through the wall before then, he might not even finish the race.

# 54

## NEVER GIVE UP

*June 12, 2015*

Casey stared down at the second envelope. Everything had gone so well over the past year that she had almost forgotten about Emma's surgery. As she thought back, though, she could still remember the horrible feeling the day her ophthalmologist informed them Emma would go blind within a month without a transplant.

It was bittersweet to hold that envelope now. On one hand she was so unbelievably grateful that Emma didn't lose her sight. But on the other, she knew it meant that another child had lost their life.

*Dear Recipient,*

*I apologize for the formal salutation, but at the time of writing I do not know your name.*

*I was informed at the time of donation that the recipient requested to be notified of the donor's name when legally possible. I requested that they allow me to reveal the name of the donor through this letter, but I do not know if they will oblige. If they do, though, I am sure one of their employees is proofreading this to ensure I don't say anything too crazy. So, hello to you as well, sir (or ma'am).*

*I will not take up much more of your time. For one, I am sure you are extremely busy. But mostly because I have already had to stop writing this letter several times.*

*I want to start off by saying thank you. I believe that my daughter found purpose in her short life, and you have helped extend that purpose even though she is gone.*

*It's strange because when I first sat down to write this letter my heart was overflowing with words. But as I sit here with the ink pressed against the blank white page, it seems as though I have already exhausted those thoughts. So, instead I will cut straight to the chase.*

*My daughter's name was Grace Lynn Wilder, and I loved her with all my heart, and yet that love was eclipsed by something as simple as her smile.*

*Before she passed I made her a simple promise. I told her that no matter what I would never give up.*

*I would not be so presumptuous to ask you to also keep that promise, though I have a feeling you will.*

> *With the love of my daughter,*
> *Her father, Benson Wilder*

Casey's hands trembled as she held the letter in front of her. She closed her eyes, choking back a startled cry. But the sob rose up within her like a wave in the midst of storm. Then they crashed as she fell to her knees with nothing but the deafening silence of her tears.

# 55

## TOO FAST

Parker ran to Coach Melvick as the runners came screaming by into lap eleven. He shoved into their mentor's view the stopwatch he held.

"Don't say it," Coach said.

"But Coach…" Parker insisted. "They're two seconds ahead of the collegiate record."

Coach Melvick looked over at Parker. "Are you fucking deaf, boy?"

Before Parker could answer, Coach ripped the stopwatch out of his hands. He looked at his clipboard and then back at the stopwatch. *Son of a bitch was 2.7 seconds ahead of the record.*

"All Ben has to do is hang back like he usually does and just burn these guys at the end." Parker said.

Coach shook his head as he looked over to the runners as they neared the first turn of lap eleven. Ben had dropped back to eleventh and was tucked deep inside a pocket of runners. Coach kicked at the ground and divot of grass and dirt went flying. Then he walked back over to Parker, handed him the stopwatch, and sat down on a green and yellow fold-out chair. *It was a good try, kid. The track is just too fast today.*

"What's he doing?" Parker asked.

Coach grunted something incomprehensible as he took his hat off and ran his hand through his graying hair.

"Coach, what's he doing?" Parker said again.

"Not now, Parker. Go flirt with one of the trainers or whatever you usually do."

Coach felt a tug on his left shirt sleeve and looked up to see Parker tugging on it like a five-year-old. He watched Parker's head move from right to left, watching the runners come out of turn two and into the backstretch.

Coach slapped at Parker's hand that was still tugging.

"Coach—" Parker started again.

Coach Melvick stood up. "Holy shit, boy. What do you want?"

Parker pointed to the runners as they passed on the opposite side of the field and Coach Melvick turned around.

"Well, I'll be damned…He knows he can't out-kick Keven Robinson. So he's going to run at such a furious pace that there is no kick for anyone."

"How does he know that?" Parker asked.

"Because I told him."

# 56

## PICK UP

*June 12, 2015*

Casey wiped the tears from her blurry eyes as she rifled through her purse for her phone. She was throwing stuff all over the living room, looking for it.

"There you are!" she exclaimed. She slid the screen to unlock and found Ben's number under her favorites list. She waited a second and the phone started ringing.

"Pick up, pick up, pick up, pick up…" she said in rapid succession.

She held the phone away from her face for a moment and looked at the time. It was 5:11 p.m. on the east coast where she was.

She put the phone back to her ear. It rang once more, then went to voice mail.

"You've reached Ben, but I'm away from my phone. You know what to do at the beep."

"Shit." Casey said. "Shit, shit, shit." This was her last hope of stopping him from racing. If he only knew about Emma and Grace …

She didn't want to leave this on voice mail, but she had to take a chance that he'd hear it. So, she waited for the beep.

"Ben," Casey said, trying to calm herself. She held her hand over her chest as she breathed deeply.

"Ben, I don't know how to say this.

"I got this letter in the mail today about the donor from Emma's corneal transplant.

"*Ben,*" she said for the third time. "The letter is from you. The donor…it was Grace." Casey paused, not sure what else to say.

"I know we didn't leave things on good terms. And I'm sorry. But if you get this message, please don't take a chance with your life and run today. Call me back, please. I love you."

Casey's phone rang instantly and she just about dropped it trying to answer.

"Hello, hello?" Casey said, almost yelling into the phone.

"Hey, are you watching this?"

Casey hung her head. It was Nikki.

"Nikki, I'm sorry, I can't talk right now."

"Are you at least watching Ben?"

Her question confused Casey.

"No. What? He doesn't race until 5 p.m., which puts it at like 8 p.m. our time."

"Casey, turn on ESPN."

Casey ran over to the couch and grabbed the remote. She turned on the T.V. and flipped to ESPN.

The phone fell from her hand as she took two steps closer to the screen.

"Casey? Hello? Casey?" Nikki said.

Casey didn't hear anything as she watched Ben run. Out in front of everyone.

# 57

## Fading

*June 12, 2015*

As he rounded the last turn Ben didn't see the gap between him and Robinson. But he could see her hair, the deep brown color of an autumn leaf. He could see her aquamarine eyes, as clear as the shallows of an untouched ocean. He could see her smile at the end of his arms like every little girl should smile.

He didn't feel his heart beating 220 beats per minute. But he could feel her fingers wrapped around his.

He ran at a furious pace, pushing beyond the limits of himself. And though he didn't hear the crowd go silent in disbelief, he could hear her voice echo throughout his mind.

His chest heaved uncontrollably as he gasped for breath and his muscles tensed to the point of tearing. The end was coming, the finish line fast approaching until at last he stepped through the solid white ribbon.

It was only pure instinct that Ben stopped running about twenty feet past the finish line. People began running towards him, but his ears were ringing and vision was blurring. He suddenly felt the entire weight of his body again and fell to his knees.

The silent stadium erupted and the announcer's voice reverberated over the track. "Ladies and gentleman. It is still being confirmed. But…" The announcer hesitated at the gravity of what he was about to say. "Benson Wilder of the University of Florida has just become the first collegiate runner to break the 5000-meter world record."

Ben could barely hear the words over the incessant pounding of his heart, but they meant absolutely nothing to him as he looked up at the clouds. He tried to speak when he felt hands around his shoulders, but couldn't.

The image of his daughter faded once again, and in her place he saw Casey's short blonde hair. He felt her soft touch as a breath of wind whispered past him. And then a second later he collapsed.

# 58

## HEAVEN

*2 years earlier, June 9, 2013*

"Do you think everyone goes to heaven?"

These questions had been getting harder over the last few weeks. People all too often underestimate the intelligence and forethought of five-year-olds.

Ben looked down at the little girl. Her small hand wrapped inside his. *It makes my heart hurt when she asks me questions like this.* "I like to think so," he said.

"Do you think I'll go to heaven?"

It took everything he had to fight back the single tear that began to form behind his eyes. "Sweetheart. You're going to be fine. You don't need to think about things like that right now."

"I know. But, just in case. Do you think I will?"

"Of course."

"What about Baby Bear?"

Snuggled against her right side was a hand-stitched brown bear. He looked down at the bear. Along the right side of his neck was two inches of black string, where he had added some stuffing recently. Ben thought if he could show her Baby Bear could make it through surgery that she would too.

"I think he'll be there too."

"And you'll take care of him if I can't?"

"We'll take care of him together. How does that sound?"

Before she could answer, the door swung open and Dr. Sanchez walked into the room. "And how is my favorite patient doing today?"

Grace smiled. "I'm doing good, but can you have a look at Baby Bear?"

She held out the stuffed animal as Dr. Sanchez walked around to the other side of the bed. He took his stethoscope out and placed it on Baby Bear's chest in several places. "Mr. Bear seems to be in excellent health."

"Good, because he's recovering from surgery," Grace said pointing at the row of stitches on his neck.

Dr. Sanchez leaned in closer. "I see that. And someone did a very fine job with the sutures."

"That was my dad."

"Well, your dad did a very fine job. And speaking of your dad, do you mind if I borrow him for just a minute?"

"Sure. I think we're going to take a nap. Baby Bear is tired." Dr. Sanchez wrapped his stethoscope back around his neck and smiled.

"You and Baby Bear get comfy, and I'll be back in just a minute to tuck you in for a nap," Ben said.

Grace moved to her left enough so Baby Bear could lie on the pillow next to her as Ben followed Dr. Sanchez into the hall.

When the door clicked shut behind them Ben quickly asked, "Is everything alright?"

Dr. Sanchez leaned against the wall and very matter-of-factly said, "We found a heart."

# 59

## GONE

*June 12, 2015*

"I'm sorry, miss, we can't release patient information to non-family members," the woman from Sacred Heart General Hospital said.

"Can you at least tell me if he's alright?" Casey asked.

"I'm sorry, miss."

Casey already knew the answer to her next question, but she asked anyways. "What about a message? Can I leave a message for him?"

"I'm sorry, miss."

"Okay, Casey said," knowing the woman was just following the rules. "Thank you."

She hung up and tried Ben's phone again, but this time it didn't even ring.

* * *

When Ben next opened his eyes there was a blurry darkness all around him, except for one small light in the distance that was getting closer and closer.

Then he heard a noise that sounded like a muffled voice. And then another. His faculties were still adjusting.

The white light was gone, and suddenly his ears were working and he could hear the voices clearly.

"Parker, if you shine that damn light in the kid's face again, I'm going to take that phone and—"

"Coach?" Ben asked, trying to blink away the blurriness. Ben closed his eyes again, and when he opened them, Coach Melvick and Parker were standing over him.

"You're going to be okay, kid," Coach said.

Ben looked down to see himself in a striped robe. He went to move his arm, but the IV cord tugged lightly. "Am I in the hospital?"

"Man, you were out cold," Parker said.

"What happened?"

"Well, you came from behind to break the world record, and then in the immortal words of Martin Lawrence, you passed the fuck out."

Coach Melvick slapped Parker on the back of the head with a rolled-up newspaper.

"Coach, what the—" Parker said, grabbing the back of his head.

"Do you have any idea how stupid you sound?"

Parker started to say something.

"Do not answer that," Coach said. "Just go get the nurse, and let her know Ben is awake."

"Alright, geez." Parker said. Then he looked at Ben. "I'll be back in a minute, don't go anywhere."

Ben laughed as Parker walked out of earshot.

"You have any idea how stupid that was?" Coach said.

"It was your idea to sprint the last two laps!" Ben said.

"Not that. That was a stroke of genius that won you the damn race. I'm talking about the fact that your little boyfriend told me that you also happened to pass out last week on a run."

"I didn't think it was anything," Ben lied.

"You didn't *think* is right. You got *lucky* it was nothing."

Parker returned with the doctor and nurse following.

"We'll be in the lobby," Coach said to Ben. "Let's go, Parker."

The nurse walked over to where Coach Melvick had been standing and read off the vitals on the screen above Ben. The doctor checked his eyes with a small light as he listened. "Sounds good," he said, and then the nurse walked back out.

"I'm good to go?" Ben asked.

"You were technically good to go about six hours ago," the doctor said. "But I imagine you needed a little nap after that performance today."

"And you're sure I'm okay? Like my heart and everything."

"You are good to go Mr. Wilder. Did a full work up while you were resting and it didn't reveal any major cardiac problems."

When the news fully processed, Ben, relieved, slumped down into the bed further. He was fine.

"So, then why did I pass out?"

"It's hard to say exactly. It's not uncommon in extreme athletes like yourself. They're called benign faints. Your blood sugar was a little low and you were a bit dehydrated, but nothing out of the ordinary. The nurse will be in in a bit, and you can get out of here."

# 60

## DEAD

*June 12, 2015*

Getting out of the hospital wasn't exactly as easy as the doctor made it out to be. About an hour later the nurse finally came back, and then it took another thirty minutes to finish up paperwork. By the time Ben got to the lobby it was close to midnight, and Coach Melvick and Parker were both passed out, sitting upright.

Ben walked over and kicked Parker's chair. "You guys planning on spending the night here or what?"

Parker wiped the sleep from his eyes and looked up at Ben. "Apparently the fastest man in the world needed nap time?"

Ben ignored the question. "You know you have drool on your shoulder, right?"

Parker stood up and tossed Ben his duffle bag. "Let's go, the girls of Florida await our return."

Coach Melvick was standing by the door. "If you ladies are done chatting, I'd like to get the hell out of here."

Ben followed Parker and Coach out to a cab that was waiting. He sat in the back next to Parker and unzipped his bag. He pulled out his phone, but the screen was black. He tried the power button several times, but it was no use. His phone was dead.

\* \* \*

When they got to the airport the plane was sitting alone on the tarmac. A man in a navy vest and matching hat escorted them down the runway towards the plane.

"Good morning," the stewardess said as Ben made his way up the airstairs.

It was just past midnight and still dark out, so technically it was still morning. "Morning," Ben said. A few steps later and his teammates all started chanting. "World Record, World Record, World Record."

Ben looked around. The plane was empty except for the men's and women's University of Florida track team. They kept chanting until Coach told them all to shut the hell up so they could go home.

# 61

## In Her Eyes

*June 13, 2015*

Ben woke to a flight attendant lightly tapping on his shoulder. "Seats up and seat belts on, please," she said.

Ben hit Parker on the shoulder until he woke up. "We're landing," he said.

Parker yawned and stretched his arms.

"Hey, what time is it?" Ben asked.

Parker looked down at his watch. "Eleven forty-five a.m."

It felt like they had been traveling for days and it still wasn't even noon yet.

It took another thirty minutes to get their bags and grab a cab. When the yellow minivan pulled up, Parker walked his bags to the back and hopped in through the sliding door. "You coming?" he said, looking back at Ben.

"I'm going to grab the next one. I got something I need to do, man. I'll catch up with you later."

"Alright, man. Good luck," Parker said, knowing exactly where Ben was headed.

* * *

Thirty minutes later Ben paid the taxi driver and got out of the car in front of Casey's house. He slipped his backpack over his left shoulder, picked up his duffel bag and walked up the driveway towards her front door.

The garage was shut, and he didn't know if she was off today, worked today, or was possibly asleep preparing to work tonight. He also didn't know exactly what he was going to say to her. And based on their last conversation there was a pretty good chance she may not even talk to him.

His heart was beating slow but heavy as he sat his bags by the door. He knocked distinctly three times, and the sounds careened off the plastered garage wall and disappeared in the wind.

Ben looked over to his left where the curtains were drawn, but saw no movement. He turned around and looked back down the driveway. Even though it was looking to be at least six hours until she got back home, he was about to sit down and wait for her to get home. Then the door opened.

Ben turned around and saw Casey. She was wearing navy blue sweat pants with the words "CAL BEARS" written down one leg in gold, along with one of his gray workout shirts that fell around her frame three sizes too big. Her hair was pulled back with several strands on each side hanging loose, and her nose and eyes were red with tears.

Before Ben could say anything, she leapt towards him, throwing her arms around his torso and burying her head in his chest. This was not the reaction he was expecting.

"I thought you were dead," she said, her voice muffled by his shirt.

Ben ran his hand over the top of her head, brushing back several strands of hair.

"What?" Ben said. "Why would you think that?"

Casey leaned away from him a bit and looked up, still keeping her hands on his waist. "I saw you collapse after your race. And the broadcasters didn't know what was happening. I tried calling your cell, but it kept going straight to voicemail. Then I tried calling the hospital and they wouldn't tell me anything about you because I wasn't family."

Ben ran his hand across her forehead, tucking a loose strand of hair behind her ear. "I'm so sorry," he said. "I didn't know. I didn't even think you were going to watch the race. I didn't even know if you would talk to me when I got here."

"Of course I would talk to you. Why wouldn't I talk to you?"

"I thought...the way we left things...I don't know."

"That was just a fight," she said. "Assuming you're not going to do anything stupid like that again."

"That's what I wanted to talk to you about," Ben said. "The USA Outdoor Championships are in two weeks."

"You can't be serious," Casey said stepping away from him.

Ben held his hands up in front of him. "Casey, just let me explain. The moment before I collapsed, I honestly thought that was it. I thought I had traded everything just to hang onto to the memory of Grace a little longer. I thought I would never see you again.

"And then I woke up in the hospital. The doctor told me they had run a bunch of tests and that I was just severely dehydrated and probably a little overstressed."

"What about your heart?" Casey asked.

"I talked to the doctor. There is absolutely nothing wrong with my heart."

Ben could see the concern still etched across Casey's face. "On the plane ride home all anyone wanted to talk about was the possibility of making the 2016 Olympics. I never imagined I would make it this far, and now I'm potentially one race away from qualifying. But…" Ben paused. He stepped closer to Casey and took her hands in his. "I won't do this without you. I can't."

"Two conditions," Casey said.

"Anything," Ben said.

"Tomorrow you come down to the hospital and get a second opinion from Dr. Hasara."

"Done."

"No more ignoring my phone calls. I don't care if you're passed out in the hospital or not," she joked.

Ben smiled. "I would never ignore phone calls from Casey Anise Taylor." He raised his hands to her face and leaned in to kiss her.

Her hands clung to his, holding him there for several seconds. "Now come inside and cuddle with me until I fall asleep. I have to work tonight."

"Yes ma'am," Ben said. He grabbed his bags and followed Casey towards her bedroom. He sat his bags down and slid off his sandals.

Casey was already in bed curled up under the sheets. Ben lay down behind her and wrapped his arm around her waist, intertwining his fingers with hers.

"Can I ask you something?" she said.

"You can always ask me anything," Ben said.

"If you don't want to talk about it I understand," she said "But, do you not want to talk about Grace?"

"What about her?" Ben said.

"I mean about the voicemail and everything."

"What do you mean?"

Casey lifted Ben's hand off her and turned around to face him. "The voicemail I left you yesterday."

"My phone was dead when I woke up in the hospital. I still haven't even a chance to charge it yet."

Casey shot up. "You haven't checked your phone since before the race?"

At Casey's worried expression, Ben grew confused. And what did this have to do with Grace? "No, why? Did something happen?"

Rolling out of bed, she walked over to her dresser. She picked up the handwritten letter and walked back to the bed, handing it to Ben.

He took the folded sheet. "What's this?"

"This came yesterday in the mail. I think you should read it."

"Okay," Ben said. "You're kind of freaking me out, though." Ben unfolded the letter, and immediately recognized the block-faced letters written in all caps. He read through the same words he had written over a year ago. The words he had written just weeks after losing Grace.

A single tear streamed down his face and landed on the paper. Suddenly he felt like he was back in another race. Everything around him stood still and was silent. He saw Casey's lips move, but didn't hear a word she said.

"Ben," Casey said. "Talk to me."

He closed his eyes and retreated back to his most precious memories of Grace. The first time she called him "Dad." Pushing her on the swing set in their backyard. Telling her endless stories at bed time.

His thoughts were finally interrupted by the sound of the front door opening.

"Stay here. I'll be right back, okay?" Casey said.

He nodded, but walked toward her bedroom door. From there he could see Casey saying goodbye to the mom of one of Emma's friends.

Ben couldn't take his eyes off Emma as she walked in and sat her pink and yellow owl backpack on the dining room table. She turned towards the couch, but tripped over her left shoe lace that was completely untied. Her head missed the coffee table by just a few inches as she fell to her hands and knees.

Casey and Ben both moved towards Emma. "You okay?" they said in unison.

Emma nodded. "This stupid shoe lace won't stay tied."

"Did your mom ever teach you about the magical double knot?" Ben asked.

Emma looked up at Casey and then shook her head.

"Would you like me to show you?" Ben said.

"Okay," Emma said.

"Okay, go ahead and tie your shoe like you normally do."

Emma recited the rhyme as she tied her white laces. "Over, under, around and through, meet Mr. Bunny Rabbit, pull and through."

Sitting there on the floor next to Casey, Ben thought back to all the times he had felt a familiar presence in Emma. All those times he had seen Emma.

She looked up at him as he began to pull her laces into a second knot, and it wasn't until that very moment that he truly saw the secret in her eyes.

# ABOUT THE AUTHOR

Wesley Banks was born and raised in Bradenton, Florida. He graduated from the University of Florida with a Bachelor's and Master's degree in Civil Engineering. After spending over 7 years building movable bridges from Florida to Washington he decided to focus on his true passion: writing.

Wesley recently moved to Oregon to get back to the great outdoors that he loves so much. He lives with his wife Lindsey, and his two dogs Linkin and Story. Most of his time these days is spent writing, with as much rock climbing, hiking, or skiing as he can fit in.

Author Page: WesleyBanksAuthor.com

# Note from the Author

I sincerely hope you have enjoyed reading this book as much as I enjoyed writing it.

If so, I would love for you to do two things:

1. Leave a review on Amazon telling what you loved about the book.
2. Come find me at WesleyBanksAuthor.com and let's connect. I love catching up with my readers.

Printed in Poland
by Amazon Fulfillment
Poland Sp. z o.o., Wrocław